GAME SEVEN

GAME
SEVEN

a novel

Tom Rock

Printed by CreateSpace, an Amazon.com company.

Queries for the author can be sent to:
GameSevenNovel@gmail.com.

ISBN-13: 978-1517109998
ISBN-10: 151710999X

You know who it's for.

PART ONE

CHAPTER ONE

It's like being a gynecologist.

That's Scott Findle's answer when someone asks him what it's like being a sportswriter. Being the guy who gets to travel to the games and hang out with the players and stay in nice hotels and watch baseball for a living. People have their own ideas about the job based on Oscar Madison or that Raymond on TV, but those guys mainly just loaf around as unrealistic versions of the profession. Besides, they were columnists, not beat reporting grinders like Scott. So whenever someone finds out he is a sportswriter – at a cocktail party, on an airplane, any time he had to fill in the "occupation" blank on a form – they always ask what it is like.

No one asks teachers what it's like. Accountants, firemen, nurses. They know that. Or have a pretty good idea. But a sportswriter? Who covers baseball? As long as no one invited the astronaut or the cowboy, Scott was pretty much guaranteed to have the coolest job in the room.

So he told them. But he played with them first.

"It's like being a gynecologist," he'd say.

Editors and critics told him his writing contained too many similes. He liked them. They helped make sense of a convoluted world. So he stuck with this one.

"Every guy thinks how great it must be to look at it all day, stare at it and dissect it and discuss it. But the truth of the matter is, after a while, it becomes just a job. Sometimes even a chore. A day-to-day slog. You used to spend every spare minute thinking about it, but now? When you get home after a long shift? It's the last thing you want to deal with."

Wait, are we talking about baseball or ...?

"You spend your life trying to understand how it works, the function of each part, the mechanics of it all. Tearing down the mysteries and the aura that drew you to it in the first place. So by the time you have a real handle on it, a true working knowledge of the processes and pieces, and you get to the point that you can confidently call yourself an expert, the exhilaration it once stirred in you is replaced by a clinical coolness. It no longer moves you. The magic is gone."

Yeah, I don't think he's talking about baseball anymore.

"You see a lot of bad examples, too. They're not all gems. In fact, most of them lack the poetic beauty that's so often projected in things such as movies and bulky, glossy magazines. Those are idealized versions, polished and coifed into a luster designed to draw you in and make you fantasize. The reality is much less clean and crisp. Far less manicured."

Ewww? I think?

"Yeah," he'd sigh, "being a sportswriter is just like being a gynecologist. Except, of course, no one asks Doc if he has two extra tickets for next weekend's big Pap smear."

It may be an exaggerated truth, but it is a truth. The best way to cure a love of baseball is to become a sportswriter and cover it. Scott found that out.

Maybe, he thought, it's because we know what we're writing is pretty meaningless. In the big picture, anyway. All of this importance is foisted upon the games and the contracts and the rivalries and the rules and the records and the traditions and the cheating and the legacies and the arrests and the asterisks and the backstabbing and the bullshit... sometimes it feels as if we're the only ones who realize it's not that important. Big deal! A bunch of overpaid athletes who represent one city (and who invariably are not from that city) can beat a similarly assembled group of transients from another city. And what? Fewer people starve? Wars end? Lives change?

Even the terms sportswriter use amused and baffled Scott. Ball and play and field and park and game – it's the vocabulary of first-grade recess. We fill the pages and the websites with those words and others, he thought, but they're empty calories. The sports pages are the potato chips of the newspaper. Betcha can't read just one!

It's the Sportswriter's Lament: Every one of them, no matter how old, lies in bed each night staring at the ceiling until it moves, wondering what they want to be when they grow up. When they get a real job. When they can do important things. For most of them, the when never comes.

The good news is, it's not permanent. The crankiness and cynicism and just being a miserable prick -- it can be reversed. All of it. Scott Findle found that out, too. Eventually. And the cure is the damnedest thing.

It's the game. Being able to see it again for what it is. When it flashes something new and exciting. When it becomes salvation.

Amazing Grace, how sweet the crack of the bat, that saved a wretch like me.

Whenever folks want to hear a story – if, that is, they stuck around past his gynecological riff – Scott tries to oblige. He has a bunch handy, kind of a Greatest Hits collection. The one about the shortstop and the manager's wife stuck in the elevator with no clothes on until the fire department had to rescue them. The clubhouse attendant who replaced the detergent in the visiting laundry room with blue dye, forcing the road team to run to a nearby Sports Authority to purchase replacement uniforms for the next day's game. The classic in which the players faked a murder in the clubhouse that was so real, the rookie from Arkansas not only called 9-1-1 to report the crime but confessed to the heinous act when the police showed up. The eccentric outfielder who splashed a few drops of Visine on the barrel of his bat before he walked to the plate so it could see the ball better.

Mostly, though, Scott learned that people want to know about the action. The games. They want to be reminded of what they already have seen: The towering home runs and the throws from the corner and the diving stabs of screaming ground balls up the middle. They want their memory of watching it to be validated. To be told that yes, it actually happened that way, even though they were sitting in a living room miles – sometimes thousands of miles – away from the play. You weren't duped. You don't misremember.

Which is why, eventually, it comes to this:

Say, did you cover that World Series?

It's pointless to ask "Which one?" There is simply no other World Series that could be called *that World Series*. It's the one between the Cubs and the Red Sox. The one that went to Game Seven and never came back. The final one played at Old Fenway before the new ballpark opened the following spring. The one that crippled the sport it was supposed to save, divided a nation, closed down a city, sent troops to the battlefront, tore up the Constitution of the United States of America, and helped decide a presidential election. Which one? That would be insulting.

So, yes, Scott covered *that* World Series. And everything that went on around it. He was at the epicenter of the action and he even played a minor role in some of the drama (although that part was quickly relegated to footnote status). It was the mixing of America's two great passions – sports and politics – and Scott was right there in the blender with all of it.

He smiles and tosses out a few well-worn anecdotes about the Series when prompted. Nothing too revealing. Anyone who lived through it already knows the narrative, and those who have been born since undoubtedly have heard the tales. It's impossible, in the confines of a casual conversation, to encompass all of it. Even the several books that have been written about the Series, they did a good job of covering the basics, highlighting the drama, breaking down the circumstances that led to what many believed was a low point for the sport from which it could never again ascend. They manage to capture some of the tensions and some of the emotions and fear and uncertainty and chaos that swirled in those strange days.

But none, Scott knew, came close to telling the whole story. His whole story.

He was 46 years old when the World Series began. By the end of it, he'd come to find out what he wanted to be when he grew up.

A late-October snowfall on the North Side of Chicago is not unusual. A late-October baseball game there, however, is a rarity. And when those first pretty flakes began clinging to the defrocked branches of ivy that grew on the outfield wall of Wrigley Field toward the end of Game Four of the most-watched, most-anticipated World Series in a generation, the visual was stunning. Scott even noted the time the snow began, writing 10:07 in the upper right corner of his scorecard and drawing a crude snowflake next to it. Really it was just an X and then another X and another, all at different angles. Not too artistic.

The important part – the Scott part – was the 10:07. He'd developed a habit of noting the exact time of key plays, important decisions, potential turning points. Baseball is not beholden to a clock; its rhythm is measured in outs and innings, not minutes and hours. To correspond the significant moments of a game to the timing of real life felt as if it bridged the gap between the two a bit. Or maybe it separated them further. Scott wasn't sure. He just liked it. It was a bit of a gimmick he picked up as a young writer when he first listened to Vin Scully's play-by-play of Sandy Koufax's 1965 gem.

It is 9:46 p.m. Two and two to Harvey Kuenn, one strike away. Sandy into his windup, here's the pitch. Swung on and missed, a perfect game!

His notebooks were filled with times. Most of them proved to be inconsequential, and he assumed that marking the time it started to flurry in a World Series game would be just as meaningless. Weeks later, when he looked back, that would be the beginning. That's where it started.

That was the thread that stuck out of the sweater just enough to draw attention to itself, subtle enough that it should be ignored but stubborn enough to be brushed at. Then played with. Then pulled. And pulled. Until the whole thing unraveled.

It was an attractive snow, he recalled. Most early snows are.

In January, snow is a 300-pound uncle after a turkey dinner, revoltingly unbuckling its belt, taking up two and a half of the three seats on the sofa and snoring above the volume of the television. It is a charming nuisance, accepted as the way things are, but a nuisance.

By March, snow has overstayed its welcome. Its white flakes are dulled to a sulky gray, its havoc piled up at the edges of driveways and parking lots. Just melt already! Go home, winter, you're drunk!

October snow is refreshing. It dances across lawns, a 5-year-old girl in a pink tutu, accompanied by innocence and frivolity and mischief. October snow smells fresh, makes people smile. Scott smiled.

He enjoyed Wrigley Field. It was a time machine, transporting its guests back to a simpler time with hand-operated scoreboards, bullpens in foul territory, batting practice cages under the outfield bleachers and brick walls that were padded only by the ivy that grew on them each summer. The accommodations were just as quaint. No giant scoreboard for high-def replays. The seats were designed to fit fans who'd never been exposed to Super Big Gulps, 30-minute pizza deliveries and fries with that. In the late 1980s, it was the last big league stadium to add lights for night games, though many of the regulars and the traditionalists – one and the same most often – much preferred the day games. There were strict rules and civic codes that were rigorously enforced on the use of the lights, which stood in six bright bays, three of them perched atop each baseline.

There has never been a better way to spend a Tuesday afternoon in July or August than in the bleachers at Wrigley, soaking up the sun and beer, barely paying attention to the action on the field below as breeze-aided dingers soar over your head. During those sun-drenched afternoons, the out-of-town games that were to be played later in the day were all lumped together on the broad green board just to the right of centerfield and behind the slope of bleachers. Letters were positioned diagonally to encompass all of them:

Such disdain. Wrigley couldn't even respect night games enough to spell the word correctly. The ballpark was built on the abandoned grounds of a seminary, but not even God could argue that the space was not put to better use when Wrigley Field was constructed in 1914.

That's not to say all Cubs fans watched their baseball in such a stone-aged manor. In the years prior to the Series, a family of high-rises had sprung up on Waveland and North Sheffield Avenues with the express purpose of eavesdropping on Cubs games from outside the stadium. The buildings were designed with balconies, bleachers, bars, food courts, big-screen televisions, even souvenir stands. It was everything a fan should have expected from a 21st century visit to a baseball stadium – minus, of course, the baseball stadium.

Wrigley sat about 41,000 fans. Close to 22,000 more could be squeezed into the seating areas across the street. Often the high-rise seats cost more than the ones closer to the actual game. In Chicago, watching a ballgame had never been about watching the ballgame.

Antiquity had its place, and the old-timey feel of the ballpark was more of a draw than the often hapless team that called it home. Eventually, cents became more important than sentimentality and it became clear that Wrigley Field had to change with the times.

The Cubs were owned by ChiLock, a money-lending company based in Chicago that paid little to no attention to the baseball aspects of its investment but kept a keen eye on the bottom line. ChiLock did not appreciate the pirating of its product by those "entrepreneurs" across the street from the stadium. Add to that the lost revenue from games that were rained out – there was an average of four postponements each April alone due to inclement weather – and the shareholders knew what they had to do. They voted to construct a retractable dome over Wrigley Field. The stadium itself remained mostly intact. The Board of Directors understood it was their greatest asset. But fiberglass sheathing was to be built around and over the existing structure. It would block the view from the renegade seats across the street and allow the Cubs to play in whatever weather faced them. ChiLock insisted that on most days the roof would be open and the experience at the ballpark would be exactly as it had been for the better part of a century – more or less. But when rain or snow or other unforeseen elements threatened to interfere with the baseball, a shell could be stretched out over the stands and the playing surface to allow for perfect conditions.

That shell was not completed until the spring after the World Series, however, so it was useless when the snow began to fall on Wrigley that night. And when it continued to fall through the next day.

CHAPTER TWO

Scott enjoyed a morning run on game days, particularly on the road. It was more of a trot than a run, never very fast, just enough to get the heart rate up and burn a few calories. If he could map a course around the stadium, that was even better. Running around the perimeter of a ballpark as it awakens, shaking off the previous night and preparing for the long day ahead, was always one of Scott's favorite experiences. The smell of stale beer kegs being hauled out with deep clunks and the high-pitched clank of the fresh ones rolled in, the sounds of the lawnmowers and sprinklers echoing through the empty cathedral, the power-washers scraping the grime and gum and goop away from the outside sidewalk so the stadium would be ready to present itself anew to the thousands of fans who were on their way.

Secretly, Scott always hoped that one day he might stumble upon a crime scene during those runs. He could be the jogger who found a few drops of blood on the side of the road – hardly enough for a zipping motorist to notice – and followed them into the woods to discover a body. It'd already be dead; Scott didn't want to deal with the messiness of having to resuscitate anyone in his fantasy. He'd carefully move around so as not to disturb the crime scene while dialing 9-1-1 on his phone-slash-GPS-slash-camera-slash-jukebox. Maybe he'd even snap a few pictures. For the authorities, of course. And Facebook.

He wouldn't be the main focus of the story in the papers the next day, but he'd be mentioned. And old friends who remembered him as a tubby slacker would call up or text and say they noticed his name in the news.

So, you're running now, Scott?

"I try," he planned on saying with forced bashfulness that he often rehearsed during the runs. "I've done a couple of 5Ks, a couple of 10s."

Wow! Good for you!

"Well," he'd say, patting his gut, "you gotta do something."

On cold mornings, or mornings after late-night games that went extra innings, when it was hard to force himself out of bed, it was this possibility that pushed him out the door. He couldn't have lived with himself if another runner had found his body, his crime scene, on his route, while he was lazily dueling with the snooze button.

Which is why he was so disappointed when he pulled apart the drapes of his hotel room the morning after Game Four and saw the streets and sideways covered in snow. His morning run was relegated to the treadmill in the Marriott exercise room, the smell of chlorine from the adjacent swimming pool punctuating his foul mood. At least he knew – or thought he knew – that there would be no baseball game that night, no chance for the Red Sox to clinch the series in five. It would give him one more chance to gallop around Wrigley the following day before heading home for either Game Six at Fenway or a championship parade through Boston.

By the time Scott's taxicab pulled up to the press entrance of the stadium, its tires crunched six inches of snow. No fans were hanging out in the nearby bars. There were no early lines for player autographs. The city sounds were dampened by the still-falling frozen precipitation. Wrigleyville – the residential area around the ballpark that bustled on typical game days – was as desolate and abandoned on this particular October 26th as it was on, well, just about any other October 26th for as long as anyone could remember.

There is no more empty feeling for a baseball writer than showing up at a park knowing there will not be a game played that day. This one had yet to be postponed officially, but it was just a matter of time.

As Scott walked into the press work room – essentially a storage room at Wrigley that had been emptied out to accommodate a few rows of tables and chairs, a couple of power strips and a weak wireless Internet modem – he was met by Sy Galoosh, the head of media relations for Major League Baseball and the information man for The Commissioner.

"Play ball?" Scott asked Sy.

"We don't know yet," Sy responded, although both men were aware there would be no baseball that night. "Say, Scott, we need a pool guy. You interested?"

Pool reporters are used when it is impractical to have the entire press corps do an interview or squeeze into an area. When the umpire blows an important call (or the rare occasion when he needs to justify the right one), he is typically interviewed by a pool reporter. That representative of the media will conduct an interview or observe a situation, transcribe the quotes, write a description of the events, and disseminate it to the rest of the reporters, who then write it as if they themselves were there.

Normally, Scott knew, it is a gigantic pain in the ass to be the pool guy. The responsibility is usually right up against deadlines, on top of the reporter's own writing that needs to be done, so the extra drudgery is not appreciated. And there are always ingrates and grumblers who snipe about the wrong questions being asked or the wrong details included.

But this was during the day and Scott figured it was a good way to score some points with The Commissioner and his voice box, Sy Galoosh.

"What are you thinking?" Scott asked Sy.

"Ever been to the Weather Balloon?"

The two men walked through the tunnels beneath Wrigley. Most of the stadium had the smell and flavor of an antique store – a charming mustiness that is earned only over decades. They walked silently through the empty, narrow hallways, past the closed door of the visiting locker room, past the umpires' room, past the grounds crew's storage area, until Sy Galoosh came to a sudden stop at a heavy metal door that had been painted green. He knocked twice, then turned the doorknob and pushed it open.

It was a tiny room, no bigger than a typical bathroom in a middle-class home, with little to no space to move around. But every square inch of it was stuffed with either technology or nerdy-looking moles squinting at the machines to decipher what the computers were trying to tell them.

"Scott Findle," Sy said, announcing the guest as the room ignored him, "you know The Commissioner."

"Of course," Scott said, stepping into the room and brushing up against one of the mole people jockeying the computers to shake his hand. "Good to see you again."

In actuality, they'd never met. Scott knew that. He also figured The Commissioner didn't.

"How have you been, Scott?" The Commissioner replied, keeping up the farce of familiarity with a pat on the shoulder.

"Thanks for coming down."

"Where are we?"

"This is the Weather Balloon," The Commissioner said. "This is where we monitor the meteorological conditions of the day, and it helps us determine whether or not we'll be able to play baseball."

"You do know there's a big patch of open space just on the other side of this wall," Scott said skeptically, pointing with his thumb toward the playing field. "You could just go out there and see what the weather is like."

He regretted his cynical reporter's attitude almost immediately but decided to play it out. Clearly The Commissioner and Sy wanted him to see something. He could at least make it slightly uncomfortable for them.

"Right," The Commissioner said. "But this gives us a chance to see what the weather will be at game time. For instance, Melvin here was just telling me about a potential window this evening in which we could have two hours to play some baseball."

"Maybe an hour and 45 minutes," Melvin squeaked.

"I think we can find two hours," The Commissioner said.

Scott still wasn't quite sure what he was doing there. He looked at Sy.

"We just wanted to be as transparent as we can be," Sy said. "In case we have to postpone tonight's game. Or we try to get it in. Either way."

"Of course you'll postpone tonight's game," Scott said. "There's a half of foot of snow on the field outside and another inch coming down every hour. I don't need all of these computer screens to know that. You should call this game right now."

Just as Scott finished the words "right now," another man barged into the room and the crowded space suddenly was too intimate for comfort. People wiggled to avoid inappropriate contact with each other and looked up at the ceiling to avoid breathing into the ear of the man beside them.

"Skip, we have to get this game in," the man said wrathfully.

It was Roger Fleiss, head of sports programming at the network carrying the World Series and enjoying the best ratings in more than a decade. Skip, of course, was The Commissioner.

"I know," The Commissioner said. "We're trying to."

"We have to play this game," Fleiss again implored.

"I understand, Roger. But there's snow and it's going to keep snowing."

"So shovel it."

"Shovel it?"

"I don't care if you have to get out there yourself with the flimsy little ice scraper that came in your rental car and push every inch of snow and slush off the face of this field, we're having a goddamn baseball game tonight."

Skip's head nodded and his shoulders sunk. He was a tall man, not thick but with a powerful slenderness. He had been the owner of a team several years ago, even made it to the Series one year, but there just weren't enough fans to support a franchise, and when baseball contracted, he lost his club. As a consolation prize, and for falling on his sword, the other owners bought him out and named him Commissioner. The result was a man worth billions of dollars with a job for the rest of his life. In most cases, he acted that way, too. He was a bumbler, a chronic mis-speaker who rarely made it through a public appearance without tasting his own size 13, but he always at least presented the air of authority and confidence.

The lashing he took from Fleiss cowered him, though. Scott had never seen The Commissioner so powerless.

"Well," Sy said, intervening on behalf of his emasculated boss, as was his job description, "that is an option. And we're keeping it open."

Fleiss tried to spin toward Sy, but he bumped into Scott on the way. These certainly were not the Friendliest of Confines, made less so by the hostility. Fleiss squirmed past Scott to go face-to-face with Sy, who instinctively looked up at the fluorescent lights to give Fleiss enough room to deliver what was sure to be a furious verbal assault.

"Do you know what we have tomorrow night?"

"The debate," Sy said.

"The fucking presidential debate. The last fucking presidential debate. So, do you know what that means we can't have tomorrow night?"

"A baseball game," Sy said.

"A fucking baseball game!" Fleiss roared.

"We think there's a two-hour window this evening beginning at around 9," The Commissioner said. "Maybe we can get a few innings in. Maybe five. Maybe enough for an official game."

"What?" Scott chirped, incredulous. "You can't have a World Series decided by a shortened game. The Red Sox are a win away from the title. Having them do it in five innings would be a disgrace. Besides, have you seen a World Series game lately?"

He turned to Fleiss.

"There are so many commercials in your broadcasts that you couldn't play two innings in two hours, never mind five."

"Who the fuck are you?" Fleiss barked.

"Scott Findle," he said.

"Who the fuck is Scott Findle?"

"He's a reporter," Sy said. "From Boston."

"Write this, Scott Findle," Fleiss spat. "If this game is not played tonight, I will make it my life's work to ensure that no baseball game is ever again played on a major network and that any future World Series will be banished to some basic cable Siberia like we did to the NHL and that stupid play-in game for the NCAA Tournament."

Fleiss turned toward The Commissioner, again brushing through Scott to get there.

"And you," he said, pointing his finger in the face of The Commissioner, "you'd better get this game in. Figure it out. Or you're going to have to call the candidates and explain to them why their last chance to impress the American public is going up against the biggest baseball game in 20 years. 'Cause I sure as hell ain't."

Fleiss stormed out of the room, pushing past both Scott and Sy to get there, then slammed the heavy metal door that hid the Weather Balloon from the rest of the world.

"That window," Melvin said, "is closing pretty quickly. Now it looks like we'll have about 20 to 30 minutes without snow."

"Christ," The Commissioner said.

Sy put a hand on Scott's shoulder.

"Obviously," he said, "this is all off the record."

Emerson Ott stood with his hands covering his face for so long, he easily could have been mistaken for falling asleep, and if he did not stir soon, one of the few posts higher than Senator -- the presidency -- would escape him. The klieg lights that focused on him made his brow drip, and even without his suit jacket on, his armpits were perspiring through his Oxford. While he stood frozen in his sweat, a small group waited patiently in the darkness of the auditorium at Arizona State University until he finally spoke through his hands so his voice was both muffled and echoing.

"Kyrgyzstan?" he asked into the microphone, then opened his eyes, dropped his arms to the lectern in front of him and looked around the room.

"Sir," a male voice blurted through the near emptiness, "what did we say about ending statements as a question? This isn't a game show."

"Fuck. Right, right. Kyrgyzstan," he said, then shouted. "Kyrgyzstan!"

"Excellent."

"Kyrgyzstan! Kyrgyzstan! Kyrgyzstan!"

He started pounding his fist on the lectern.

"Kyrgyzstan! Kyrgyzstan! Kyrgyzstan!"

"Yes sir," the voice said, trying to regain control. "No too much excitement, though. We're not attacking them. And now ... who?"

Ott stopped pounding and yelling. His lip curled as he thought.

"He's a president, right?"

"Yes, sir."

"I can picture his face. Long nose. Gray hair."

"Very good, sir."

"It's ... *crap!* ... Atta boy or Atom Boy ..."

Ott continued searching the files of his brain for the answer. His voice tried to lead him there.

"President Alm ..."

"Alm ..."

"Almazbek ..."

"Almazbek Atom Boy?"

"Almazbek Atambayev," the voice said.

"Almazbek Atambayev ...," Ott repeated, trailing off, groping for another syllable or two.

"No, sir," the voice chided. "That's it. President Almazbek Atambayev of Kyrgyzstan."

"Right, right," Ott said, trying to gather himself.

"So let's try the whole thing over again. Julie?"

This time a woman's voice rang out through the darkness.

"Senator, which of the former Soviet Republics do you see the United States needing to build a closer relationship with in order to establish an American foothold in the bridge between Russia and Iran?"

"I'm glad you asked," Ott said, "because just last week I met with President Almazbek At-am-bay-ev of Kazakhstan -- no, wait, shit -- Kyrgyzstan. Gah! Who cares? The fuckheads in this country know more about Kardashians than Kygyzstanis. Nobody knows who these people are."

"Governor Brandt will," the male voice said.

"Bullshit."

"Sir."

"Bull," Ott said with a pause. "Shit."

"Sir!"

"What?!"

Ott squinted into the sea of blackness through the blinding spotlight, but all he could make out was the rectangular glow of some kind of electronic device being held up by one of his aides.

"Sir, you have a phone call."

"Unless it's Atom Boy -- or Brandt calling to concede -- tell them we're busy. The final debate is in just over 24 hours and we have to nail this down so I can watch the Cubs game tonight. It's Game Five and they're already down 3-1."

"Sir, it's The Commissioner."

"Of what?"

"Of baseball, sir."

Ott stood up straight. He nodded and licked the salty sweat off his lips with his tongue and ran his hand through his silver hair before wiping his perspiration-soaked palm on his pant leg. "Oh."

On his way out of the stadium later that night, with the game officially postponed until the following day, Scott again ran into Sy Galoosh, just as he had when he arrived.

"How'd it go?" Scott asked.

"Pretty shitty," Sy said.

"You had no choice," Scott consoled. "That window never showed up."

"No, I guess it really never was going to, either."

"Did The Commissioner call the big boys?"

"The candidates? Yes."

"And how'd that go?"

They answered together: "Pretty shitty."

Sy and The Commissioner were on a conference call for most of the evening with the two candidates -- Emerson Ott and Henry Brandt -- along with their campaign managers, representatives from every network news department plus Roger Fleiss, members of the bipartisan Commission on Presidential Debates, and the president of Pepperdine University, where the final debate was to be held. There was so much yelling and screaming during the conference call that it was impossible to tell who was calling The Commissioner a spineless cocksucking coward and who was calling him an anti-American scumbag traitor. The president of Pepperdine, it turned out, had an exceptionally colorful vocabulary.

Finally, after all parties involved had spewed their venom and taken a moment to catch their breath, they tried to decide what to do. It takes months of negotiation and interaction and give-and-take to design a presidential debate. Now, just about 24 hours before the final one of the campaign was scheduled to begin, they had to try to come up with alternative plans.

"Move the debates to earlier in the evening," Fleiss suggested. The other network heads who repped news departments and not sports howled at the idea of losing their easy prime time ratings grabber by airing it at 6 p.m. on the East Coast, 3 p.m. on the West.

"Why don't you push the game back an hour?" one of the cable news channel honchos offered, but Fleiss bristled for the same reason his own idea was shot down. Start a World Series game at 10 p.m. EST? Impossible.

They bandied about ideas, but each was met with resistance. They could tape the debate and air it at another time -- but that would leave the networks able to edit it, and who was to say that Fox News' broadcast wouldn't look different from MSNBC's? They could push the debate back a day -- but the Great Hall at Pepperdine already was booked solid for the next week. Every idea -- from shortening the debate into a *Jeopardy!*-style answer-and-question format complete with buzzers and wagering to having the candidates debate from the broadcast booth at Wrigley Field during the game -- was proposed and then summarily rejected.

The Commissioner, at one point, had the temerity to suggest that the game and the debate both go on, head-to-head, at the same time. That was met with another round of indecipherable insults hurled at him from all parties.

In the end, they came to the only reasonable conclusion, absurd as it was. The debate was canceled.

"I suppose the American people have heard enough from us," Ott finally said, sounding a bit relieved to have ducked the final test of his presidential timbre and have a chance to watch the game. "I mean, we've been at this for almost two years now. If there's anyone whose mind will be made up between us by something that is said on a stage tomorrow night, I'm not sure that vote should even count."

The light chuckle at the end of his statement was met by silence. Then it was Brandt who closed the call with a diatribe against The Commissioner.

"This is the problem we have in this country," Brandt said, grandstanding for the conference call to the point that there were audible here-we-go-again groans from other participants. "We put important things that are important to our democracy on the back burner and bring the inconsequential to the forefront. Mr. Commissioner, you are a lowly man in charge of a lowly pursuit, and somehow you and others here believe that your game is more significant, deserving of more attention, than the basic elements and framework of our government. It is with disgust in my heart and bile in my mouth that I agree to this arrangement. It is, indeed, a sad day for America."

Sy Galoosh laughed as he finished relaying Brandt's speech to Scott.

"What's so funny?"

"Well, we hung up after the conference call, and about 15 seconds later, the phone rings again. It was Brandt. He wanted to know who he needed to talk to about getting tickets to the game for himself and some staffers."

CHAPTER THREE

At some point in their illustrious lives, Thomas Edison, Henry Ford and Harvey Firestone all established winter homes in the town of Fort Myers, Florida. Edison's home, which was called "Seminole Lodge," actually was designed and built in Maine and then transported to Florida on a fleet of sailing schooners in 1886. It was re-assembled on 14 acres of riverfront property.

When Scott took over the beat in Boston, it was the Red Sox who came down from New England to be re-assembled each winter. The team had held its spring training in Fort Myers since the early 1990s, so every February, players and reporters began filing in from around the country to start the journey that would become the upcoming baseball season.

Scott's first trip to Florida was three years before the Sox made it to the Series against the Cubs. The outgoing beat man, Ray Giffords, had been doing the job for 32 years but was retiring in April. He took Scott out for a few drinks on their first night together in The Fort with the purpose of passing along a few pointers, a few phone numbers, and a few words of wisdom. It quickly turned into a bitch session.

"The Professor," as he was known in writing circles -- a nickname that as much paid tribute to his knowledge as it derided his abundant willingness to share it -- suggested a place called Gator Bites Tail and Ale. The Professor showed up wearing a pair of white slacks with white shoes and a white belt, and a navy blue rayon shirt with the top three buttons separated by a sea of chest hair. It was a ridiculously dated look. At Gator Bites, he fit right in.

It didn't take long for The Professor to begin his dissertation on the state of sports journalism.

"It's all bullshit," he railed. "Nobody cares about quality anymore. When I started in this business, you could spend a day working on a story. Now, you still spend the day working on it, but the public gets to see every step of the production. First you tweet it. Then you write it for a blog. Then you write it for the Web. By the time it's polished and in the paper, it's already old."

Like you, Scott thought but held his lips closed. Instead he nodded politely.

"And this guy Lattimore," The Professor continued, about to skewer the new sports editor. "What's his problem? I get six or seven phone calls from him a day. I've been doing this job for 32 years, Scott. I know what I'm doing. I don't need to have my hand held by some twerpy bean-counter in the office."

The Professor called down the bar for another Dewar's and water.

"I knew it was over when they gave me this," he said, flipping his iPhone onto the oak. "That's where they got me. That's when they really had me by the balls. There was no escape. Did you know that in 1987, I went seven weeks without once touching base with the office? Seven fucking weeks. I just sent my copy each night, they put it in the paper the next day, and that was that. No fuss. None of these phone calls. No emails. Oh, those goddamn emails."

The Professor took another hit from his refreshed glass. "And what's with the stupid way he ends his emails, anyway? JKL? What the fuck is that about?" "I think it's his initials," Scott said meekly. "Jack K. Lattimore. I don't know what the K stands for."

"Probably 'Cocksucker,'" The Professor said.

Scott chuckled.

"I think that starts with a C."

"He's so interested in changing the way things have worked for decades, he'd probably spell Cocksucker with a K. Jack Kocksucker Lattimore."

Another slug of Dewar's for The Professor.

"Ever hear the one about the writer and the editor who were stranded in the desert?" The Professor asked. Scott hadn't.

"Well, they're marooned out there for days and days just wandering around. Until finally, thankfully, they come across an oasis. The writer jumps into the water and drinks it and splashes it all over himself. He turns around to look at the editor. The editor is standing there and he's dropped his pants and he's urinating into the pool.

"'What the fuck are you doing?' the writer asks him.

"The editor looks him straight in the eye. 'I'm making it better,' he says."

The Professor finished his drink and pushed himself away from the bar.

"That reminds me," he said. "I gotta piss."

"Make it better, Professor!" Scott called.

He walked to the back of the restaurant, past the unmanned It Will Be Our Pleasure To Seat You sign and through the proper dining area that was just as vacant. Scott remained at the bar by himself and surveyed the surroundings, both physically and professionally.

He'd been covering baseball in Kansas City for more than a decade, but mostly as a backup wingman, a second-fiddle, the guy who wrote the easy sidebar or stuck his head into the visiting clubhouse to see if there was any news there. Now he was back in his hometown of Boston and the main guy on the Red Sox coverage. It was a whole new level of responsibility. And clearly, as The Professor pointed out so eloquently, the job itself was changing.

It was JKL who hired Scott and brought him home to Boston when his life was in shambles. Scott had been raising his son, Ryan, by himself since the divorce (if, by "raising," you meant finding a babysitter for him six nights a week during the school year). There were, Scott supposed, worse ways to spend an adolescence than having a father who covered big league baseball for a living. Plenty of perks and swag, road trips in the summer, chances to meet the players. Not a bad experience for a 12-year-old kid. Scott had a rule against Ryan collecting autographs, which he knew were a burden to the players, but he allowed the occasional selfie just as long as no one complained. They never did.. To the contrary, the players often tagged themselves in Ryan's pictures on social media sites that Scott couldn't remember, never mind pronounce. Sites such as SpLYD and KnUdiT. Scott had to remind himself that many of the players were closer in age to Ryan than they were to him. It was sobering.

Moving back to Boston meant being close to his parents, who could pitch in with the child-rearing. They were getting older, but at least they were family, and that would assuage some of Scott's guilt. Scott also thought it would be helpful for Ryan to leave Kansas City, to get away from all the old friends and neighbors who knew them when they were part of a three-person family. On that point, Scott realized he was projecting more than protecting.

So Scott had some gratitude for the editor. He was willing to give him a chance. Scott figured he could deal with overbearing. He had been married to the Queen of Overbearing. Besides, that's what voicemail is for, right?

He spent the next several minutes inspecting the patches from various law enforcement agencies around the country that adorned the back wall of the bar area and the collection of gator heads mounted above the mirror, each wearing a different cap from a Red Sox minor league team.

There also was a black-and-white picture of Henry Ford and Thomas Edison standing side-by-side on the beach. Scott was quickly learning how deeply the community held tight to its link to those two, even though they didn't do much work in Florida and basically just came to town for vacations over the summer. Those houses were now historical landmarks and museums and, when the Red Sox were not training there, the biggest tourist draw in town other than the beaches.

Scott wondered how many nights over the next six weeks he would spend at this establishment. Maybe he wouldn't be back. There had to be other places in Fort Myers. He gave a quick scan of the restaurant and saw no other writers. They had to be somewhere else. Hopefully, he thought, there *is* a somewhere else in this town.

The Professor came back and ordered another Dewar's.

"I don't mean to scare you, Scott," he said with a belch he was barely able to hold in. "Sometimes, though, I feel like the blacksmith with a shop full of horseshoes watching the first automobiles roll down the street past me. Things are changing. Quickly. Too quickly. What used to be valuable isn't anymore. Now a writer makes his name on this stupid thumb machine" -- and he reflexively pushed his iPhone a few inches further away from him -- "more than the ability to do his job properly.

"I'm just glad I'm getting out now," The Professor professed. "Man, I'd hate to be chained to this line of work for another couple of decades."

They both drank to that, only one of them condemned to its truth. Scott knew he was becoming disenchanted with his job, but he still had a ways to go before reaching The Professor's level.

"Boy, I'm really feeling these drinks," The Professor confessed. "All of a sudden, too. I'm starting to feel a little light-headed."

"Well, you've had three of them," Scott said. "Did you eat?"

"I had dinner at the hotel. But I usually ..."

The Professor grabbed onto the edge of the bar to steady himself. Scott jumped off his barstool to brace him from behind. It was only when The Professor's body leaned away from the bar that Scott noticed the red splash across the crotch of The Professor's white slacks. It looked as if a plate of spaghetti had fallen into his lap.

"What the fuck is that?" Scott said with alarm.

The Professor looked down. His face was turning pale. The stain grew deeper and began spreading.

"I ... I don't ... ehh."

And with that he collapsed into Scott's arms.

"Doctor!" Scott yelled. "Somebody get a doctor!"

The bartender asked what was wrong and looked over the bar as Scott placed The Professor down on the sticky floor as gently as he could. Senior citizens hitting the deck in Florida is not cause for much concern. But when he saw the pool of blood soaking into the white synthetic fabric of the pants, the barkeep turned his head away quickly, gathered himself and went to the phone to call for an ambulance.

Scott had no idea what to do. He could wait for help and just try to be as comforting as he could, but that might mean The Professor would lose more blood. He could die on the floor of the Gator Bites Tail and Ale.

Scott decided he needed to go in.

With a deep breath he unbuckled the old man's belt, unbuttoned the slacks and slid the zipper down. It was worse than Scott imagined.

The Professor was also a Commando.

Not only was he going *sans* underwear for the evening, but blood was now spouting from his scrotum. Scott could hear the gasps -- and a few giggles -- from the onlookers who had gathered from nowhere and were gawking at the old man on his back. He stood up and grabbed a handful of cocktail napkins from the plastic holder atop the bar and, after once again bracing himself with a deep breath, shoved the clump of absorbent paper onto The Professor's geysering genitals. He turned his head away in disgust and did the only thing he could remember from the first aid classes he took years ago as a Boy Scout.

He applied direct pressure to the wound.

"Don't let go!" the EMT told Scott as they dashed from the Gator Bites Tail and Ale to Lee Memorial Hospital in the ambulance that the bartender had summoned. "Just keep squeezing! Pressure!"

Scott was very glad The Professor was unconscious for this escapade, but walking out of the bar next to a gurney that carried the old man whose pants were shorn away from his waist, with his hand plunged deep into the most personal depths, was mortifying. More than one customer at the scene had taken a cellphone video of their departure, and Scott was sure it would go viral by the time they arrived at the hospital. That was when he came the closest to letting go of the goods.

Anyway, he wasn't sure exactly how hard he should be squeezing. A firm grip seemed as if it may do more damage than good. A loose hold seemed a little too playful. Scott tried oscillating between the two while trying to find the proper tension to his clutch on The Nearly Nutless Professor, but quickly realized the horrible mistake that was. Eventually he settled on a pressed palm instead of a full clutch. Best not to involve the fingers at all, he figured.

When they pulled into the Emergency Room driveway at the hospital, Scott again tagged along beside the gurney, the Dutch Boy with his finger in the dyke. They were ushered furiously through the hallways, past the waiting room and the billing station, into a triage room.

"What do we have here?" a doctor -- Scott assumed he was a doctor; he had on a smock and a mask, so he could have been anyone -- asked.

"He just started bleeding," Scott said.

"And you were together when this started?"

"Yes," Scott said. Then he wondered what the doctor was asking. "No."

"Which is it?"

"We were together. But not *together* together."

"Uh-huh," the doctor said with a hint of disbelief. "Well, let's take a look then."

Scott removed his hand and the blood-soaked cocktail napkins from The Professor's crotch for the first time in nearly half an hour. At first it seemed as if nothing was out of place. Scott even leaned in to get a better look. But then the wound reopened and a fresh spout of blood squirted him in the face.

"Whoa!" the doctor said, reaching in himself this time to stop the flow. He turned and looked at Scott, who simply stood there with The Professor's ball blood running down his face. He was in shock.

"Jessica," the doctor called, looking around the room until he saw a familiar nurse. "Can you help our friend here get himself cleaned up" -- he tilted his head toward Scott -- "and when you come back in, I'll need a suture kit."

When The Professor awoke in his hospital room the next morning, both Scott and the nurse were there.

"Where am I?" he asked with the confusion of a much older man.

"Lee Memorial," the nurse said.

"The hospital," Scott clarified.

"What happened?"

"As far as we can piece together," the nurse said, "when you went to the bathroom at that bar last night -- the Gator Baiter, was it?"

"Gator Bait Tail and Ale," Scott again clarified.

"Right. When you went to the bathroom, you must have zipped up a little too quickly and lacerated your scrotum. We found some flecks of flesh caught in the metal teeth of your slacks. It left a..." – the nurse eyed the chart to be sure -- "six-millimeter slice on the exterior of your..." -- again to the chart -- "left testicle."

The Professor's mouth fell open and his eyes shot downward to the bulge of bandages that now adorned his midsection.

"Don't worry," the nurse said. "Everything is going to be fine. Good as new. Or as good as it was yesterday before all of this. All of the damage was external. It took 22 stitches to close the wound. You'll have to come back in about two weeks to have them taken out. I have a handout for you on caring for the wound. But I'm afraid your boys will require some rest."

"Didn't you feel it?" Scott asked. "How could you not feel it?" The Professor blushed.

"You should be glad Scott was there," the nurse said. "You could have lost so much blood that you could have died. Scott saved your life."

"How?" The Professor asked.

Scott and the nurse looked at each other.

"Forget it," The Professor said. "I don't want to know."

CHAPTER FOUR

Sitting in the press box for Game Five, Scott's mind began to wander. He didn't mind. He found he did some of his best writing when he allowed his thoughts to stray. As long as they stayed somewhere close to the basepath of his story, he was confident it was a productive exercise in creativity. He always wanted to be more of a baseball poet more than a baseball writer, and allowing his consciousness to stroll off just a bit was usually effective to that end.

On this night, his thoughts were with Ryan.

Scott conceded he was far from a perfect father. But the waterboarding he most regretted in the psychological warfare known as parenting came on the Little League baseball fields. He hated watching his son play baseball, which was the mathematical impossibility of two positives (Ryan, and baseball) equaling a negative (Ryan and baseball).

Scott found the games exciting, particularly as Ryan grew older and the players matured in their physical abilities and awareness of nuances. Sometimes a team would turn a double play, and every once in a while a runner would be astute enough to take an extra base. Or be even more astute and not try when not trying was called for. In baseball, sometimes the smartest plays are the ones you don't make; swallowing the ball instead of forcing a crazy throw and chucking it away, or staying at first instead of trying for a double and ending a rally.

But Scott's detestation of Little League baseball came from one emotion that welled up inside him every time Ryan walked to the plate.

Guilt.

Was it he who was sending him there to fail? Because without a doubt, Ryan would fail. Scott thought it would be clever to name his son after his favorite pitcher, even if he did flip-flop the names. Nolan seemed more inconspicuous as a middle name anyway. Maybe that was the jinx right there, saddling the boy backwards. Or maybe having the father who wrote about baseball made him more of a target.

Scott would sit in the stands -- or more often stroll deep down the leftfield line, away from the other parents, under the guise of having a better angle but really to get away from their incessant chirping and hovering -- and find himself jealous of the other fathers. They got to come to games with at least the hope that their son would succeed. They had a chance. Put the ball in play in most Little League games and it tends to start flying all around the field. Pretty soon you're standing on third, having driven in two runs after a dribbler to the second baseman, and tossing the game ball happily into the air on the way back to the car after the game.

Scott found himself especially jealous of the parents of the kids who could play well. It was an ugly jealousy. It must be easy for them, Scott would think, going to all the games to watch their darlings succeed. Strike out the side over and over from the mound. Their chest must swell every time the opposing coach moves the outfielders back, or tells the shortstop to stay awake during his at-bat. He could only imagine the confidence those parents had every time a ball was hit in the direction of their precious All-Star.

Scott loved his son. Dearly. And there were things Ryan did well. At least Scott tried to tell that to himself.

"He'll find his thing eventually," Scott would say to those who asked what his boy was up to and came at him with lists of activities that their children didn't just participate in but excelled at. Whatever belts in karate. High something at the piano concert. Super advanced platinum or some other made-up-sounding status from the dance recital.

Playing baseball just wasn't one of those things for Ryan. And that would be fine in almost any other circumstance. Scott joked that Ryan inherited athleticism (which is to say none) from his mother. At least he tried to joke about it. Deep down, there probably was more blame than comedy in his barbs. But Ryan also inherited something from Scott, which was a love of baseball, as well as an inherent awareness of the geometry and timing and history and beauty of the sport. It was a heartbreaking combination of traits to be given from one's parents (and not the only time, it should be noted, that this couple's inability to align themselves would create turmoil). The result: A child simultaneously encumbered by the desire to achieve in a particular realm and the inability to ever do so.

It was easier when Ryan was younger. The games were less competitive. Winning wasn't as important. Everybody struck out. Or walked. As he grew older, though -- 10, 11, 12 -- the players developed. The ones who didn't mostly dropped away from the game to find something else to occupy their springs and summers. Scouts. Swimming. Girls. Video games. Drugs.

Ryan was one of the ones whose skills didn't develop, but he stuck with it. At first, Scott tried to see the nobility in it, the honor that comes from standing in front of a dragon knowing that your suit of armor is about to be turned into a Dutch oven.

"If you want to build character, you have to start out with some char," Scott would say. Although the pun worked better on paper because of the spelling, Scott would still say it. But did he believe it?

He got it in principle. After a while, though, it became tough to watch the flambé and not feel bad for the cherries.

Ryan would walk up to the plate with a focused look in his eyes. "This time," Scott would say to himself, and he could tell Ryan was thinking the same. He wasn't in the stands to hear them, but there must have been groans from the other parents when they saw Ryan coming up, particularly if the team was in the midst of a rally or needed a spark. Scott tried hard to quell the groans in his own head, but sometimes they bounced around so furiously, they made his scalp itch.

Some players have naturally pretty swings. Lyrical loops in their bats as they wait for the pitch to come in; a terse, meaning-ful stride; hands that glide through the hitting zone like a Samu-rai sword. Robinson Cano from Ryan's generation. Dale Murphy from Scott's. Scott would say that Ryan had the prettiest non-swing in the league, which was his way of finding something to compliment him for and dashing a little humor over his misfor-tune. But it was the truth.

It began by placing the bat under his left arm as if holding the morning newspaper, and squatting down catcher-style. There he would rub his hands in the dusty dirt of the field and spit the seeds that he had inserted into his mouth while waiting on deck. Once his batting gloves had collected enough of the surface, he would stand up tall, eyeing the pitcher, and clap his hands to-gether once, but loudly, to create a cloud of debris in front of him that he would walk through. The way Mick Jagger comes out on stage amid the effects of a smoke machine. Part LeBron

James, part Maximus from "Gladiator." It was fairly dramatic, and if you hadn't already been to a few games, you'd be wondering why this kid was hitting last in the order.

He would dig into the batter's box with his back hand extended toward the umpire, in complete control of the pace of the game. One, two, three twists of the right foot, then the placement of the left gentle as an egg in a nest. The left hand would reach out with the bat to tap the far corner of home plate, proving to himself he could reach the outside paint. Then there was the twist of the left wrist and the bat would spin in front of him, counterclockwise, quickly coiling, making a full circle and then some before landing in front of his right shoulder. This is where it would be joined by the right hand that had been traffic-copping the umpire. His head turned to the pitch at this point, his attention now focused on the baseball. A quick tap of the aluminum bat on the back shoulder and it would spring up, a sunflower straining for the last rays of a late August evening. He bent low again at the knees, came up, then settled in at the perfect height; the needle of a scale bouncing before finding balance.

The pitch came to him. His front foot would slide gracefully forward, his hands would cock back, as if pulling on a rubber band to shoot it across the room. All of that power and precision. All of that beauty. His head would stay on the pitch right into the catcher's mitt. Strike. He would drop his hands, step out of the box, and take a short, slow-motion practice cut just to give a hint of what would have happened to the pitch had he deemed it worthy enough to swing at.

Move the outfield back indeed.

When he actually did swing at a pitch, though, it was as if none of the muscles in his body would act in concert. It was a flail. His left arm swung at a different speed that his right, creating an awkward dragging and pulling imbalance. The weight of his hips would lunge forward, causing that well-dug-in back foot to come off the ground. His head would shudder so violently that the brim of the helmet banged against the bridge of his nose and blindfolded him. The elegance of his stance evaporated and was replaced by gangly limbs spasming, unable to work in conjunction with each other. The result was an awkward display that never -- never, ever -- resulted in contact. He'd lift the helmet off his eyes, shake his head and look around with a what-the-hell-just-happened? expression as if he'd just been dropped off by a bus in a strange town ... and didn't even recall getting on the bus in the first place.

"Don't be afraid of the ball, Ryan!" the coach or some other parent would yell. Scott hated that the most.

He wanted to yell back that Ryan wasn't afraid. He was very brave. What other 12-year-old would face certain embarrassment and failure two or three times a game and keep coming back for more? It's running down the hallways of the middle school in your underwear. Between each period. For three straight months.

Ryan never missed a game (although Scott was sure the rest of the team wouldn't have minded if he had, particularly for the important ones). He never missed a practice. He never missed a season, enrolling in spring, summer and even fall. He only missed pitches.

Baseball is a game of failure. The great ones are unsuccessful seven times out of ten. But it's also a game of averages. Even the terrible ones succeed two times out of ten. One and a half? Ryan was the anomaly.

Every plate appearance for the last three years had ended in either a walk or a strikeout. Three years and not a single groundout, not a soft popup, nothing. No contact. At the start of every season, Scott bought Ryan a new aluminum bat, and each year he thought about saving the receipt so he could return the equipment pristine, unscathed, undented, unscarred, at the end of the season. Then his heart would break a little more, he'd throw away the receipts, and he'd think to himself: *This time.*

Scott had no idea if anyone else was aware of this streak of swings and misses. He didn't even know if Ryan recognized it, though he suspected eventually he did. Because while he walked to the plate with that stern *This time!* look on his face and the powerful, overly-embellished routine, by the time he turned and trotted back to the dugout with his head down, his optimism had turned into a wince. Not a hard one, not an especially painful one -- more as if he'd been plunked in the back or hit a flare off the end of the bat on a particularly cold day and had to shake the sting from his hands.

It was a wince of resignation. Pursed lips. Eyes squinting. Almost a smile. Almost a smile. The kind of face you make at a not-especially-sad funeral, the one for the 94-year-old who had a stroke in his sleep a week after his wife of 71 years passed away. One that says: *No, it's not wonderful ... but, (sigh), I think we all knew it would happen.*

Scott would wince back with his own near-smile, trying not to show too much disappointment. Not that it would have been aimed at Ryan anyway, the disappointment, but toward himself. Scott would wonder: Was it he who kept subjecting Ryan to this turmoil? Was it he whom Ryan was trying to impress, to please, with each at-bat and each inevitable failure?

What guilt. What frustration. But Scott dared not show it on his face, lest it be interpreted as displeasure with Ryan. And it wasn't Ryan's fault. He just couldn't hit.

It was that same wince that Scott saw on the face of Buster Sinclair over and over. Perhaps that was what drew Scott to him.

Every beat writer has a favorite player. Not like when they are kids, when stats determined heroes and hitting .300 made up for personality flaws. These relationships were much more complex, just as life itself had become.

Three years after taking the Red Sox job, Buster Sinclair, a reserve outfielder, was Scott's guy.

He wasn't a great quote -- not that anyone asked for one; he hardly played -- nor was he destined for greatness. But they'd arrived with the team the same day. His spring training signing was Scott's first story on the beat, a bond they overtly recognized at least once a month.

"Remember our first day?" Sinclair would ask, a bit dimly, a goofy half-grin on his face that showed too much top gum.

"Who are you again?" Scott would retort with his own teasing smirk. "You new here?"

"Fuck you!"

"Thanks for the quote. I'll hold on to it until I need it."

It was the same dialogue each time. Scott complained and joked about the boring simplicity of the exchange with other reporters, but he always participated with Sinclair. Like starting a game of peek-a-boo with a toddler, it became a burden quickly. But he didn't have the heart to call it off.

Sinclair was the kind of guy who took nothing seriously. He was the one who used the eye drops on his bat (not that it helped much). On his right hand from pinky to index finger he had the letters P-L-A-N tattooed across his fist. On his left hand from index to pinkie were the letters A-H-E-A. Under the last A on his pinkie was crammed in the letter D.

One of the funniest stories Sinclair told -- and he told it a few times -- was the one about his dog when he was a kid growing up in Louisiana. His parents bought the dog for him on his ninth birthday. He named the pup Stay, he said, to drive it crazy. It was an old gag, but apparently Sinclair actually did it.

"Come here, Stay!" he would yell to the poor mutt, which never knew how to respond to the command.

Sinclair had the whole press corps giggling at the idea of a nine-year-old with such a wicked sense of humor.

"Sit, Stay, sit!" he yelled. "Heel, Stay!"

The reporters chuckled with him under the warm Florida sun of training camp. Until Sinclair walked away to take batting practice or shag flies. Then they chuckled at him. All but Scott. He didn't have the heart to. He knew the wince.

He knew it as he knew the face of his own son. Because Buster Sinclair, like Ryan, was an awful hitter. Sinclair would make some contact, get a few hits, but more often than not, he'd turn back to the dugout with his bat, peeling the batting gloves from his hands like the skin off a ripe banana, looking up into the crowd but at no one in particular while making that near-smile of resignation. How many times had someone yelled at Sinclair: *Don't be afraid of the ball!*

Scott wasn't even sure exactly how Sinclair stuck with the team. He must have been able to hit at some level in the minor leagues, but when Scott looked back at the records, he saw feeble numbers that should have produced an early retirement. Instead, Sinclair was with the Red Sox. A mystery. Scott asked a scout about it once. The guy just shook his head.

"No one knows," the scout said. "But the sonofabitch can run."

Sinclair was nearly the hero of Game Five, the first one after the Series resumed following the snowstorm, and he would have been remembered not as a clubhouse prankster and not for the wince he offered after his many failures, but as an all-time favorite son of Boston had he been able to make just one play.

Such was not his calling.

Sinclair was inserted as a pinch runner in the ninth and scored the go-ahead run, dashing from first to home on a double by Jimmy Grouper that was tangled up in one of the arcane crevices along the outfield wall of the old ballpark in Chicago. He ran past the warning arms of the third base coach and slid headfirst into home plate, barely but clearly avoiding the tag of Chicago catcher Boone Flanagan. If it stood up, it would be the Series-winning run.

"Stay! Stay!" yelled Casper Gulligan, the third-base coach for Boston, as Sinclair chugged past him. It was clear on the replay that Sinclair blew through the stop sign. It immediately reminded Scott of the story of Buster and his dog. He filed the thought away in case he'd need it in the coming days.

Boston didn't score again in the ninth inning, and the game went to the bottom of the ninth with Sinclair in left, a defensive replacement, the dust and chalk from the home plate area still blurring the air in his proximity.

Scott tried to imagine what was going on in Sinclair's head, standing in leftfield now, those low lights of Wrigley that were dropped down another seven feet to accommodate the rising shell around the stadium spreading shadows around him, replaying the run home in his mind. All of the wincing, all of the groaning from the stands, all of the articles written about whether he should or should not be included on the postseason roster -- Scott had written that he would come in handy at some point and deserved a spot, while others were far less welcoming -- and there he was, three outs from becoming a hero. Now two outs. Then ...

In a matter of moments, Buster Sinclair was instantly enshrined in that museum of notoriety established for the ones whose gaffes cost their teams the big games. Merkle, Pesky, Branca, Buckner, their misdeeds became part of the lexicon. Perhaps, Scott thought later that night, the public would take pity on him more than the others, especially considering the circumstances. Those other men had managed to walk off the field after their debacles, trying hard to hold a capped head high, knowing the questions, jeers and recollections that would greet them the rest of their lives. Somewhere behind those mustached jowls in 1986, Buckner must have seen a future that had him sitting at a table with Mookie Wilson in 15 years' time, signing photographs of the moment that would forever link them. But still, Buckner was able to walk away. Sinclair had to endure the further ignominy of being wheeled off the field on a stretcher, having the game halted for 32 minutes while an ambulance and its crew drove onto the outfield grass to scoop him up, a white sheet covering his bloody face.

The strange of it was that the play wasn't even scored an error. Chicago had runners on first and third with one out when a short fly ball was hit to left. Sinclair, blissfully enjoying the final moments before his name once again became synonymous with lost expectations, charged hard to get a running start at throwing out the tagged-up runner at home, his cap rolling off his head as he hustled. He must have peeked up to see the runner, or perhaps check on a cutoff man, for just a moment, long enough to lose sight of the ball. Or perhaps it was the unnatural angle of the lowered lighting bays that blinded him. But instead of landing in the wide-mouthed glove attached to his left hand, the ball cracked him just above his left eye. The sound of bone breaking echoed above the roar of the crowd. Sinclair fell to the ground immediately. Then, for a brief moment, nothing. As if the lights went out.

Chuck Dawson, the columnist sitting next to Scott in the press box, proclaimed with a detached, unemotional syllable: "Dead." It was 10:17 p.m. Scott jotted it down.

It certainly seemed Buster Sinclair might be dead, killed by a fly ball the likes of which he'd caught so often that counting would seem foolish. Who knows when a ballplayer makes his millionth catch? His ten millionth? Does a player ever reach a billion? The only sure bet was that for Sinclair, this wasn't it.

At the moment ball and face collided, there was a shred of silence in the raucous ballpark, 40,000 people anticipating a memorable moment and wanting to be sure that, generations from now, they'd be able to tell their grandchildren they were in the park and heard the loud crack of rawhide meeting skull themselves.

Sinclair didn't have the strongest arm in the league -- his best tool and, it turned out, his demise, was his speed -- so that he was credited with an assist on the play that killed him was ironic. The ball ricocheted off Sinclair's hatless head directly toward second base. The runner who was on first had gone halfway, holding up, anticipating that the ball would be caught, and he was forced for the second out when second baseman Manny Ortega blithely picked up the ball on the bag.

But by the time Ortega turned toward home, the runner from third was crossing the plate with the tying run.

By the time Ortega turned back toward left field, Sinclair, on the ground motionless at that point, was surrounded by the centerfielder, the shortstop, and two umpires. They were frantically waving their arms toward the dugouts, imploring trainers and doctors to join them, and soon a crowd of more than two dozen hovered above Sinclair, still face-down on the neatly-trimmed grass that had itself died several weeks earlier but was painted a luscious green so it "popped" on television.

Unsure how to react as Sinclair was wheeled off the field, his body strapped motionless to a backboard, many fans applauded politely.

The Cubs won in the 11th.

"What happened to Stay?" Scott had asked Sinclair at some point on one of those warm spring days in Florida when they had a moment alone. Sinclair looked confused and Scott had to remind him.

"Stay? The dog named Stay?"

"Oh," Sinclair said. "I don't want to talk about it."

"Since when do you not want to talk about something?"

"It's ... touchy."

Scott pushed Sinclair a bit more, and eventually he relented.

Stay became so neurotic -- due mostly to his odd name Sinclair assumed -- that he sometimes wandered in tight circles for hours.

One day Sinclair and his brothers were playing touch football in the yard and Stay trotted out an open gate into the street in front of the house.

Sinclair said he noticed Stay was missing just about the same time he heard a brown UPS truck upshift on its way down his block and around the blind bend his house occupied. By the time he realized Stay was spinning in the middle of the street with the truck bearing down on him, Sinclair had time only to shout for the dog.

"Stay!" he screamed the way only an 11-year-old boy can call for his dog when he is in danger. "STAAAY!!!"

Stay finally listened. He lay down in the street on command and the truck crushed his spine. Sinclair said he ran up to the mess, got to within about 15 yards of the scene, then had to turn around, vomit and tears falling on the sidewalk. The truck driver screeched to a stop and was very upset. After a few minutes, he got back in the brown vehicle and carried forth, pulling away from the scene at a much slower pace than he had arrived.

"That's awful," Scott said, shocked by the story. "I'm sorry."

It wasn't until the next day, the day after the play and Game 5, when Scott had a chance to truly analyze what had happened, that he recognized the actual link between Buster Sinclair and his malapropped pooch. Had Sinclair listened -- and stayed -- in the top of the ninth, just as the poor dog had done, Boston might have lost the game anyway but Sinclair would not have met the fate he did.

Prior to leaving the stadium that night, The Commissioner announced that an appropriate amount of time needed to be observed before baseball could resume. Nearly everyone agreed. What brought less of a consensus was how long "an appropriate amount of time" should be.

A day?

That was the traditional period of mourning a team received if a player passed away during the regular season. It'd happened two years earlier, when Detroit's Bill Siff was shot and killed on an off-day elk hunting trip with his son, Billy Junior. Siff died on a Monday, Detroit's game against Texas on Tuesday was postponed, and the teams played a day-night doubleheader on Wednesday. The same routine had been followed for previous midseason departures. A day off for tears, play two the next day.

But those passings usually occurred on a dark highway after a game and a few too many clubhouse beers. Or in a hotel suite with empty prescription bottles littering the floor. Or, in the case of Siff, when coming between a teenager with a hunting rifle and a 12-point bull elk on a remote game ranch in north Texas.

Buster Sinclair had not only timed his death with the World Series, the sport's annual showcase, but he'd accomplished the feat on national television, leaving behind a Zapruder-like replay that spooled everywhere from the 24-hour sports networks to the daily half-hour entertainment magazine shows. A day was enough for the public to overcome the shock of Bill Siff's death. Buster Sinclair's would need more time.

So, a week then?

Well, that seemed a bit tedious. Sinclair was a fine man and a decent player despite his failings at the plate, and his stature in both categories showed a posthumous growth spurt even after he'd lost the game – or hurt the Sox's chances, which was the same thing in Boston -- by taking the liner off his head. But Sinclair definitely was not week-worthy. Presidential deaths. Earthquakes. Maybe those sorts of occasions would merit a seven-day pause before the sixth and possibly the seventh game of a World Series. Maybe.

A week would give both teams time to rest their entire pitching staffs, and with the season boiled down to a single game or two, that seemed too unfair. Baseball is all about using resources wisely today so they can be harvested again tomorrow. Wouldn't Chicago have used its bullpen differently in Game Five had it known it would have a week off? Couldn't Boston have let starter Niles Wielander go the distance if it'd known that he'd also be available to pitch Game Seven on more-than-full rest?

Speculation about what was proper ranged wildly. The morning after Sinclair's death, one callous caller to the sports radio program back in Boston suggested Game Six be played that night so Boston could take advantage of the Gipper-induced adrenaline -- win one for Sinclair! -- and not lose its focus, as it would be apt to do with a week of memorials and funerals. He was followed by another caller, just as absurd, who voiced the opinion that the series should be ended "in honor of one of Boston's all-time great sports legends" and that the new stadium being built in Boston should feature a 10-foot bronze statue of "the immortal Bruiser Sinclair." That Sinclair was not an all-time great sports legend -- he'd been with the team only three seasons and was a bench player for most of that time -- and that he'd clearly proved just hours earlier that immortality was not his game, seemed to matter little. Nor did the fact that the caller didn't know Buster Sinclair's first name.

The Commissioner announced that morning that Game Six would be played on Oct. 31, Halloween Night, at Fenway Park. That gave Scott three days in Boston without any actual baseball to cover.

But one funeral.

CHAPTER FIVE

Henry Brandt needed to duck his head while walking the hallway from the elevator to the large swinging door made of steel bars welded together -- it looked more useful for a jailhouse than a ballpark -- that led out to Sheffield Avenue. The ceiling was low to begin with, about seven feet off the ground, but hanging from it every five or so feet was a bracket that hugged more than 50 cables, wires, cords, pipes and lines. It made the clearance in this part of Wrigley Field more like six feet. At six-foot-four, Brandt stooped considerably to avoid the delicate highway of information, electricity and sewage that flowed above him.

It was a short walk from the elevator to the door, no more than 20 yards, but on the night of Buster Sinclair's death, he spent 20 minutes hunched under the infrastructure. As his advisers chatted furiously among themselves, Brandt swayed against the cinderblock wall that was painted in the team's colors.

"Sir," one of his advisers said, trying to gather the candidate's attention above the din of ideas. Unable to stop the swaying, she cleared her throat and tried again.

"Sir!"

He stopped the nervous push from foot to foot, made all the more awkward and psychotic-looking because of his hanging head tucked under those cables. He looked at the adviser for an answer.

"Felisha," he said to her, and the others halted their conversations and monologues. "Do you have an idea?"

She did not at the moment.

"Sir," she said, "I just wanted to let you know that your suit, it's ..."

The swaying against the rough cinderblocks had caused the navy blue wool on Brandt's jacket to snag and gather, with a few flecks of the dark blue paint managing to jump from the wall to the clothing. Brandt inspected the damage, which was minimal but would have worsened with each further abrasion.

"Yes, thank you, Felisha," Brandt said. "Well, what have you come up with? We have to say something."

"Just say you enjoyed the evening and you're looking forward to Game Six," suggested one of the young advisers.

"No, no, no," another said. "A man died. He didn't enjoy the game."

"Of course not," a third added. "Besides, when has the Governor of Massachusetts ever enjoyed a game in which Boston lost?"

"Good point," the original idea man said, and slowly faded to an outer ring around the candidate.

"How about something like this," another tried, clearing his throat. " 'On this tragic night, let us all pause to remember one of America's fallen heroes, a ballplayer who left this world giving his all for a team and a cause in which he believed.' "

Brandt shook his head, his eyes re-fixed on the floor despite the temporary halt to the swaying.

"Hero?" Brandt scowled. "He was a backup, for God's sake. And if he was any good, he'd have caught the fucking ball."

"Sir," Felisha said.

"Christ, we have to say something," Brandt said, his voice rising with his eyes and his posture. "I can't just walk out of here and not say something. I'm a week away from a presidential fucking election!"

"Sir," Felisha repeated, and Brandt looked directly at her. He had an exhilarating way of looking at people, Felisha had come to learn, a glance of stern optimism. It was a put-you-on-your-heels stare that said both *You can do it* and *You'd better do it*. It demanded results and yearned for success. Felisha still was shaken when Brandt gave her that look, even though it had been happening with more regularity in the last two months of the campaign. When Brandt gave that look to Felisha this time, her stomach merely flinched and she was able to regroup and offer her solution.

"Sir," she said, composure and the governor's attention again fully hers, "you should probably just keep it simple and bar-stooly. People won't be looking to you for answers tonight. But they'll be watching to see how much you are like them, and how they can relate to you. This is another of those chances to move away from the stuffiness."

Brandt remained silent, then stood straight up so his head hit the flow of cables and caused him to flinch back to his slight crouch.

"You're right, Felisha," he said with excitement that could have been drawn from the current in those wires he'd contacted. "Let's go."

Outside the stadium, cameras gathered their aim at the heavy jailhouse-style door. With a briskness that strained the hinges, it was swung open by two Secret Service agents and a flood of advisers spilled onto the sidewalk, followed by Brandt with Felisha beside him.

Governor, what'd ya think of the game? a reporter shouted as Brandt made his way through the iron door and into his Town Car, purposefully moving on but walking slowly enough to field a question.

"I think it's a shame," he said, pursing his lips briefly enough to mourn the fallen ballplayer and the fallen hopes of clinching a title, only one of which would survive to a sixth and possibly seventh game. "I thought he had it. Wow."

Brandt enjoyed the full extension of his spine for only a moment, scrunching to wiggle into the Town Car that would take him back to the hotel. It had been a long day -- one that started with a stump breakfast in Columbus, a fried chicken lunch at a VFW in Scranton, a black-tie dinner in New York and a quick flight and dash to Chicago to watch the last five innings of the World Series game. Brandt may have been running for the presidency, but there was no way he would miss a chance to see his team clinch a championship in person. Besides, Felisha had said, it was good for his image. It showed him doing things "regular people" enjoy. A Boston title could mean a two- or three-point jump in the polls, and with only a few days until the election, that might be enough to win it all.

As Brandt settled into the leather seat of the car, he looked at Felisha, whom he had waved in with him and two others. He smiled at her, flashing the softer side of that signature stare. Then he looked out the window at the crowds of fans still milling around the stadium, most retaining the disbelief that had been heaped upon them. Their Cubs were still alive, and one of the Red Sox's players wasn't.

"Shit," Brandt said, the shell of politicking left in front of the television cameras and microphones, only earnest disappointment hovering in the car like the scent of a pine-shaped air freshener. "I really thought he had it."

It wasn't until the plane swooped down low and made its final approach into Logan that Scott realized he was completing the final road trip of the season. Win or lose, the Series wouldn't be going anywhere else. Game 6 and, if necessary, Game 7, would be played at Fenway Park. A magnificent sendoff for the old ballpark. Fenway had seen more than 100 years of baseball since opening in 1912. It would see no more after this year. Thirty-five thousand seats had gone from colossal to cozy and finally, in an era of skyboxes and corporate sponsorship, confining. The new stadium, supported by a mesh of public funds and private contributions intertwined so deeply that there was no way to legitimately track either, was being built on an empty lot two blocks from the current one.

The Bratton Family had owned the Boston franchise for three generations, but when William "Flip" Bratton III died in 2002, his children made it clear the team was for sale. Boston Commodities and Merchandise, a company known as BosCAM that already had an ownership stake in everything from the Celtics to the Boston Pops, purchased the franchise outright for $900 million. The company had the foresight to buy the empty lot and a few adjacent properties before making a bid for the team. BosCAM was planning to build a new stadium for its team before it even had the team.

Throughout the summer and into the fall, the sounds of construction just outside the old ballpark -- the creaking swing of the 200-foot crane, the rat-tat-tat-tat of the welding, the blaring warning beep of the trucks moving backward that helped spring the new ballpark from the ground -- were loud enough to squelch the cheers, boos and cracks of the bats that had filled afternoons for all those years. Scott and the other beat writers who covered the team on a daily basis somehow blocked out the ruckus, became used to it. But each series, when the visiting writers would show up for the first game, they would point out the commotion and it again would become clear to the every-day inhabitants. Then it faded into the soundscape until the next team came to town and its writers griped anew.

The old ballpark was scheduled for demolition after the season. By late August a wrecking ball loomed next to the players' entrance. Someone thought it would be cute to paint the 10-ton steel ball white with red laces, and it became such a popular attraction for pictures that it had to be moved because the players were unable to file through the crowds who gathered not to see them, but the wrecking ball. It was, of course, moved to the press entrance on the opposite side of the stadium. Reporters walked directly underneath it as they went to and from work each day.

The only part of the park scheduled for salvation was the iconic leftfield wall. It had become the most identifiable trait of the team and its home, and it was decided that, plank by plywood plank, it would be dismantled and moved to the new stadium. This appeased the traditional senses of the fans in Boston, until it was learned that the wall would not be reconstructed on the new site but used to separate stalls in the restrooms.

The leftfield wall in the new stadium would not be made of wood, but plasma -- a 35-foot-high, 55-foot-long high-definition video screen had been designed for the enjoyment of the fans and showcasing BosCAM's latest technologic holdings. A marketing tagline would hover above the screen: "Win a Million Bucks If You Can Crack This Screen!" It was dubbed indestructible, and smaller living room-sized versions would be marketed to families with children or pets that had ruined so many plasma televisions in the past.

The new wall had another trick. It was a two-way mirror, so

luxury suites and high-priced boxes could be stacked behind it with a perfect, unobstructed view of the game. The view from behind the wall would not be impeded by the commercials flashing on the other side. It was one of many mistakes made in designing the new place. Charm and character were replaced by a corporate chill. It originally was to be called WorldLab Stadium after the human genetics company based in Boston plunked down $10 million for the naming rights. When the community expressed outrage at the cold tag that rang stuffy and impersonal, the name was changed -- to WorldLab Park. And when a feng shui expert suggested, upon absorbing the auras of the infield, that the baselines be shortened from 90 feet to a more symmetrical 88, the board of directors at BosCAM actually was disappointed that The Commissioner denied the request.

The decision to destroy the old ballpark was not popular. Workers at the new place would end their shift and come catch a game at the old one in the evening. Early in the season, they'd forget to remove their distinctive light blue BosCAM hard hats and would be roundly booed. By May, they either left their hard hats in their cars or stopped coming at all.

The playoffs were a call from the governor, a stay of execution (although Brandt was pro-death penalty, so not *this* governor). The old ballpark would live, at least until the team it housed was eliminated. But Boston won a one-game playoff against Minnesota to clinch one of the wild cards. Then beat Houston to in another one-game duel to determine the singular wild card. Then it won its Divisional Series against Oakland in five. In the League Championship Series, it took seven games to defeat Cleveland. For a franchise that had a history synonymous not only with failure but spectacularly epic failure, the kind of flameouts that light up the entire sky and send shrapnel raining down on all of New England, it was as if the old ballpark's will to live was superseding the bad luck that had plagued Boston's team for most of the last 100-plus years.

Scott walked off the plane into the gate area at Logan just in time to look up at the televisions blaring the morning news programs. Several other writers from other outlets were on the same flight, and they paused for just a moment as Governor Brandt's remarks from the previous night were replayed on the broadcast.

"I didn't know he was at the game," said Mike Gross, a columnist from New York who had been a traveling partner with Scott for the last few weeks after the Yankees didn't make the playoffs. They'd both started their careers in Kansas City, had known each other's families, and although their friendship wasn't as close as it once was, they had a shared history that was rekindled each time they crossed paths. "That fucking guy is everywhere."

Scott didn't move as he watched the television. He just stared at the footage of the candidate and his entourage. More so, he was staring at the entourage.

"Hey," Gross said, tapping Scott on the shoulder to make sure he had his attention as the governor entered his car with a striking brunette. "Isn't that Felisha? Your wife?"

"Ex," Scott croaked. "Ex-wife."

The words across the bottom of the screen said Brandt would be attending Buster Sinclair's funeral services in Boston in a few days. Scott knew that meant Felisha would be there too.

It was only then that he understood how Sinclair must have felt, to think he had everything lined up perfectly, and then have it all go black.

CHAPTER SIX

There were only two things that made Scott truly happy: Ryan and baseball. He wouldn't be seeing much of either of them for the next few stressful days. While the World Series came to a morbid halt, Scott had plenty of stories to report and write, but no games to cover. And because of all of the peripheral work that went into filling three days of newspaper sports sections without an actual game, he wouldn't have time for Ryan. That was why he brought him along to the funeral, so they could at least have a few hours together even if it was on the occasion of someone else's being laid to rest.

But there was another reason he wanted him there. He needed his support.

The night before the funeral, Scott received a phone call while he still was at the stadium working. He recognized the number right away as JKL's. He was working late too.

"Hey, Jack."

"I'm calling to see if you got my text? About the email I sent you? Did you get them?"

"I did," Scott said calmly, still writing, trying not to pay much mind to the intrusion. "I figured I'd call you in the morning."

"I wanted to get this out of the way tonight," JKL said. That stopped Scott from typing and grabbed his attention. He waited for JKL to tell him what he had to tell him. Nothing.

"So …?"

"Well, this whole thing is getting big," JKL said. "Bigger than just the Series. Between Buster and with the election and everything else, I think we're going to bring in the cavalry."

"The cavalry?"

"We think you're doing a great job, Scott. We just need more boots on the ground. There are so many angles to cover."

Scott preferred working alone. It was much easier to do the work of three people than have to handle two others. His beat writer paranoia flared up when more reporters were working on the same day, a fear that something would be missed because everyone would assume someone else had it. If Scott handled everything, he'd know everything was taken care of. And if it wasn't, he would take the blame. And he was okay with that too.

"What'd you have in mind?"

"Well, we're going to send out The Professor."

Scott was relieved. He'd kept in touch with The Professor every couple of months since his retirement, sometimes checking to see if he had a number for an old-timer and sometimes just to check in. It would be good to have The Professor around for these last few days of the season. He would bring balance, perspective and calm to the situation. Scott liked him. Plus, he was no threat to Scott on a professional basis.

"That's fine," Scott said. "Good idea."

"We thought it would be good for him -- and for us," JKL said. "I'm not a big nostalgia guy, but a lot of our readers grew up reading about the Sox under his byline and we were kicking around ideas the other day when one of the news editors asked if he was even still alive. So we're dusting him off for the last game or two here."

"Awesome."

"He was excited, too. He's been following the season and the Series, so he's up to speed on everything."

"When's he coming up?"

"He'll be there for the memorial service tomorrow."

"Great."

"I'll be there, too."

"Oh. OK. Great. I'll see you there."

"Yeah."

Scott could tell there was a missing piece to the conversation. All of this could have been hashed out in an email or in the morning. Their awkward pause lingered before Scott broke it.

"Anything else?"

"Yeah."

"What?"

"We're going to add another reporter to the team as well."

This time Scott didn't give the courtesy question to snap the silence. It was JKL who shattered it.

"Fig."

The next morning they stood at the edge of the freshly dug grave. Scott had his right arm around Ryan, who turned to burrow his face into the breast of his suit.

"It's just not right," Scott said in a low, muffled moan.

Ryan looked up into his father's eyes.

"Why?" was the only syllable the adolescent could muster.

Scott had no answer for him. He inhaled the cold air and looked to the heavens. The winds coming off the harbor were stinging and his eyes, already susceptible to the accumulation of tears because of the funeral of Buster Sinclair, watered further.

They weren't the only ones at the graveside. JKL was there. He stood on the other side of the six-foot pit, across from Scott, rocking back and forth. Every once in a while he would slide part of his hand out of his overcoat pocket as inconspicuously as he could, tuck his chin into his shoulder, and glance down to check his iPhone for any new messages or updates. He was here as the sports editor, representing the paper, and baseball certainly was the biggest story these days. But the Celtics and Bruins were about to start their seasons and the Patriots had a big one against the Steelers this weekend, so he was also keeping tabs on the other sports.

Next to JKL was The Professor. Retirement had not been kind to him. In three years it seemed as if he'd aged 15. He walked with a cane now, and he tripodded heavily on it as he stood firmly planted on the consecrated ground. Maybe it was the artificial hip that caused him to lean away from JKL, or maybe it was the deep-seated disdain that had not been blunted with time.

The group observed silence appropriate to the occasion. Finally, it was Ryan who spoke up.

"This is awful," he said, peeking just over the edge of the grave. "Awful." Scott nodded and pulled him tight, back away from the hole in the earth.

"Yes," he said, then looked across the span of the grave at his two colleagues. "Somebody should say something."

"I'm not," The Professor said, shaking his head. "I hardly know the guy."

JKL sneaked another check of his iPhone, a chain-smoker palming a quick drag.

"Jack," Scott said, and it seemed to startle him from his addictive glances. "Jack, it's time. Say something."

"Why me? You know him best."

"Because you're the highest-ranking officer here. He's retired," Scott said, pointing at The Professor. "You're the boss. It falls to you."

"All right, all right," JKL said. This time he pulled the phone all the way out and gave it an unabashed inspection before jamming it back into his pocket. Sighing, he stepped forward so the tips of his muddy shoes dangled over the edge of the grave and a few pebbles cascaded down into its depths. JKL looked around at the faces one last time to size up the small group, make sure no one else wanted to volunteer for the duty at the last moment. Then he cleared his throat politely into his fist and looked down into the hole.

"Hey," he barked. "Get out of there!"

Nothing. Then a bit louder.

"Yo! Get up!"

Ryan could no longer bear watching and returned his face to Scott's suit jacket. JKL bent over and picked up a larger stone, about the size of a matchbox car, sized it in his hand, rubbed some of the excess mud from it, then threw it into the grave.

"Oof!"

"You shouldn't be there," JKL said, louder than before. "Out!"

"Almost!" a voice shouted back from below. "Just another minute!"

"No," JKL said firmly, looking around nervously to see if anyone was watching him yelling. "Now!"

"Just come up," Scott added in a quieter, more pleading way.

"OK, OK," the voice conceded.

Fig O'Leary was the nation's most well-known Gonzo journalist, following in the literary footsteps of Hunter S. Thompson, Tom Wolfe and George Plimpton. Unlike those others, however, Fig concealed his identity as much as possible. No publicity pictures. No television interviews, at least none without ridiculous black dots over his face and Darth Vader voice manipulations. He didn't want anyone to know what he looked like, he said, because one day he might become a restaurant critic. But aside from the desire to see their mugs on the backs of books and in magazines, Fig was a kindred spirit with those trailblazers.

Their kind of writing and reporting -- often more the former than the latter -- tried to reach essential truths through unconventional methods. Fig, for instance, had won a Pulitzer for his work exposing Brazilian gold miners involved with human trafficking in Papua, New Guinea. But instead of going undercover as a gold miner as one might expect, Fig paid some down-on-their-luck gauchos 100,000 BRLs (expensed, of course) to kidnap him and followed the trail that way. When it came to a story, Fig always wanted to get as close to the inner workings of the system. He wouldn't trace the exterior of the pipes to mark the trail of a flushed turd, he'd rather climb through the sewers with it to experience what it was like to be a piece of shit firsthand.

Fig wasn't a sportswriter, although his columns sometimes appeared in the sports pages. Such as the time he participated in an underground MMA bout outside Providence and wrote from the point of view of the foot that kicked him into unconsciousness. He wasn't a political writer, either, although his work often skewered those in power. Such as the one in which he proved that the state police chief was texting lewd photographs to young officers -- female and male both. By that time such actions had become nearly commonplace, but what separated this story from others was Fig's ability to prove that the pictures from the chief weren't even of himself. He'd been taking snapshots of well-endowed inmates and passing them off as his own. A blurred image of Fig's own schlong, taken by the chief during a recent

turn in County, ran on A1 with his story.
At the paper they both wrote for, Fig O'Leary was a rock star and Scott was a roadie. Not many papers employed those types of writers anymore. In fact, theirs was the only one. That the term Gonzo journalism had been originally coined in Boston -- "Gonzo" was a Southie term, Irish slang for the last man standing after an all-night bender of booze -- made the paper all the more proud to have Fig in its employ.

(There are some who believe that the term "Gonzo journalism" stems from the French Canadian word "gonzeaux," which means "shining path." In other words, the way to the truth and illumination. That may well be. But in Fig's case, it was widely accepted that the root of the term based on drinking was more on target.)

Fig was a misfit. A genius. A pervert. A drunk. A loose cannon. An embarrassment. Obnoxious. Inappropriate. Vulgar. Loyal. Ambitious. An editor's nightmare. A publisher's dream.

He was also Scott's roommate at Boston University and his one-time best friend.

And now he was trying to climb out of a grave in a cemetery, hanging on the lip of earth at his arm pits, dangling and kicking, trying to pull himself back to the land of the living, slipping back from each inch of progress, a drowning man climbing onto an overturned kayak.

"Can you gimme a lift?"

Scott and JKL exchanged frustrated glances then reached down, each grabbing an arm. They gave a silent count -- one, two, three -- then pulled from the depths of a six-foot grave the very-much-alive body of Fig O'Leary.

"What were you doing down there?" Scott asked as Fig rose from his knees, straightened his cargo shorts, dusted off his Hawaiian shirt with images of naked hula dancers, kicked sand and pebbles from between his feet and the flip-flops that we wore, and removed the white ear buds that were blaring incomprehensible music into his brain.

"Scotty!," Fig said when he was finally put together, yelling at an inappropriately loud decibel level to be heard above the still roaring ear buds. "We're working together again!"

Scott glared at his editor.

"You didn't tell him, JKL?" Fig said, noticing the awkward eye contact between the two.

"I told him -- we just didn't have a chance to iron out the details yet," JKL said.

"Well, I'm here now. Let's talk."

"What were you doing down there?" Scott asked again.

"Oh," Fig said. "Right. Well, I wanted to see what it would be like to be Buster Sinclair today. You know, walk a mile in his shoes. Spend a little time in his new home here. See what the view is from the other side."

"Buster was cremated," Scott said.

"Hmm," Fig said, then chuckled. "Well, I guess it's a good thing I didn't know that."

"Yeah," Scott said with a stern straight face. "Good thing."

"So whose grave is this?" Fig asked.

The group looked around the cemetery just in time to notice a hearse with a procession of two limousines and a dozen or so sedans heading in their direction.

"I think we should go," JKL said.

Instead of an urn, the remains of the former backup outfielder were placed in a 64-ounce plastic souvenir beer cup commemorating the World Series. It was one of those sold at the games in both cities and officially licensed by Major League Baseball. Presumably this one had not been used prior to its new calling, but a few last suds to soak up would not have upset Buster Sinclair in the least.

The cup was placed at the front of the chapel on the grounds of the cemetery, perched on the stool that once stood in front of Sinclair's locker. Not that everyone in attendance would have recognized it. Scott did the moment he walked in. How many times had Buster sat ass-naked on that vinyl padded seat talking to Scott, squeaking with each skin-sticking squirm to get comfortable, answering questions, telling stories?

The first several rows of seats were roped off, reserved for dignitaries who would be coming to pay their last respects as well as the Red Sox players. The Cubs remained in Chicago for an extra day during the three-day hiatus from the World Series, but ChiLock sent a lovely floral arrangement that stood in the corner: a large circle of white carnations laced with red roses to look like baseball stitches, and in the middle, a series of blue carnations in the shape of their mascot. Without detail, the Cubby looked more like a pixilated Mickey Mouse -- a circle with two smaller circles as ears -- than the young bear it was intended to represent, but the context led the mind to a natural ursine conclusion.

Scott and his accompanying entourage, which now consisted of Ryan, JKL, The Professor, and Fig -- they were a movie star away from the cast of Gilligan's Island -- scanned the quickly filling room for seats. They settled into a row three-quarters of the way back and sat in respectful silence. Scott was on the aisle that ran down the middle of the assembly, and as the players walked in and took their seats, some of them gave him a tap on the shoulder or noted his presence in other non-verbal ways. The raised eyebrow of grief accompanied by the lifted chin. The nod of shared mourning. The burbled lips blowing horse breaths to illustrate the exhaustion of the circumstances.

The Commissioner was the first of the dignitaries to enter, accompanied as always by Sy Galoosh and several other suits. Scott figured he would be sitting in the front row, but to his surprise, The Commissioner took a seat on the aisle, directly in line with Scott, in the second row.

Sinclair's mother and sister entered next. The Commissioner, who had just sat down, stood up and embraced them. Surely they would be sitting in the front row. But no. They sat across the aisle from The Commissioner in the second.

Scott was contemplating who might outrank the mother of the deceased in a situation such as this when five burly bodyguards with dark sunglasses and earpieces walked in and cleared a path. Scott could see the flashes from the photographers still popping outside the door as Emerson Ott, the Senator from Illinois, candidate for President, and Cubs fan of great reknown, walked in.

Ott paused briefly in front of the beer cup, folded his hands solemnly and bowed his head. Then he turned and extended his condolences to the family. Finally he shook hands with The Commissioner. Acting coy, he looked around and asked no one in particular where he should sit. "Here?" he pantomimed, pointing to the row beside the family, then the back of the room. "There?" he seemed to be asking with his gestures. Finally he spun and pointed to the row in front of The Commissioner. "Ahh," he mouthed with wide eyes as if he'd just shuffled through the refrigerator looking for ketchup and finally found it. He allowed his small staff of aides and advisers to file into the row first and then sat down on the aisle just ahead of The Commissioner and directly in line with Scott.

That left the row in front of Sinclair's family empty. It wasn't for long. Another flurry of flashes and well-dressed henchmen escorted another dignitary into the room. Scott could not see who it was, exactly, but he had very little doubt. It was Brandt.

Ryan tugged at Scott's sleeve.

"There's Mom," he whispered.

"Scott!" Fig yelled, loud enough so the congregation heard and spun around to look. "There's Felisha!"

The team chaplain gave some brief opening remarks before yielding to The Commissioner, who stepped to the wooden lectern that was elegantly carved with comforting yet nondenominational images of birds, flowers and decorative scrollings.

The Commissioner thanked everyone for coming on behalf of the family and acknowledged the two presidential candidates in attendance. He even made a joke about their rooting interests and the fact that their final debate had been canceled because of Game 5 two nights earlier.

"I'm sure neither of you wanted to miss the game," The Commissioner said with a faint smile, and some nervous, polite laughter emanated from the gallery.

"I wouldn't have minded," Brandt said with perfect timing that made the crass remark seem unbelievably appropriate. Normally a living gaffe, he managed to stick the landing on this one-liner. Of course, there were no television cameras to capture it. But Scott jotted it down in his notebook; he was here to remember a friend and bury a ballplayer, but he was also on the clock.

The Commissioner went on to talk about Sinclair, although there wasn't much to say in regard to his baseball acumen. Sinclair had left behind a mother and sister but not a stat line that could be recited with reverence at such a moment. A .554 OPS and a .251 OBP were hardly the kinds of numbers anyone would want engraved on a headstone. And talking about a player's negative WARP at his memorial service would have been wrong on so many levels.

So instead The Commissioner focused on what he'd been able to learn about Sinclair from his Wikipedia page, which he had printed out and was now reading from. Directly. It didn't disguise his source material that after every statement he spoke a number -- "He was a tuba player in his high school's marching band, seventeen"; "He donated Red Sox tickets to orphans for games on Mother's Day and Father's Day, twenty-nine" -- reading the citation and footnote markers as if they were part of the text.

After his conclusion -- The Commissioner looked earnestly at the assembly and directed them to external links and further reading materials before folding his printout in triumph -- he welcomed Governor Brandt to say a few words.

Brandt stood somberly at the lectern and expressed his condolences to the Sinclair family on behalf of the Commonwealth of Massachusetts, Red Sox Nation, and, for some reason, all three branches of the United States government on whose behalf he had no known authority to speak.

"Nothing can help replace your son, your brother," Brandt told the family. "But I want you to know that I will always be available to ease your burden in whatever way I can."

It was a sweet sentiment from the governor. But then he continued.

"For instance," he said, "we have an election next week as you may well know. And if I am elected president, one of my first acts in office will be to reduce the estate tax on after-death transfers to no more than 28 percent on each million dollars inherited. Furthermore, I hope to convince Congress to expand the parameters of tax-free posthumous gifts. Under the current administration, assets left to a spouse or a federally-recognized charity are exempt from taxes up to $5.2 million. I'd like for that benefit to include siblings and surviving parents, such as yourselves. There is no reason you should have to be burdened by the good fortune of having a wealthy son, a wealthy brother, who met an untimely passing. Thank you."

Brandt returned to his seat. The befuddled chaplain took the podium.

"Well," he said, "I suppose we should hear from Senator Ott now. Senator? Your, um, rebuttal?"

The words relieved the tension in the room and Ott bounced up from his seat, a prize fighter answering the bell. He too extended his condolences to the family just as Brandt had done, but more so, including all of the world's governments and "the people of all seven of our majestic continents, including Antarctica."

Then Ott spoke about how, if he were elected in less than a week, his Guaranteed Enrollment and Reimbursement Management program would include medical coverage for accidents such as a line drive to the head.

"The American people need to know that if they wind up like Buster Sinclair, knocked unconscious by a baseball or a horse-shoe or whatever apparatus of recreation they chose to employ, the government will not turn its back on them. We've all heard in recent weeks commercials about these so-called 'Leisure Suits' that claim that under my plan, the Guaranteed Enrollment and Reimbursement Management program, the government will seek restitution through the courts for repayment against any injury sustained during the pursuit or enjoyment of sports, outdoor activities and certain other brands of physical merriment. In fact, during the game two nights ago, the very night we were scheduled to have a debate, when the broadcast cut away and Buster

Sinclair was wheeled off the field, one of those commercials falsely denouncing my plan aired. Now, I'm not going to suggest it was a conspiracy or that Governor Brandt had any influence over the placement of that advertisement. But I would just like to reiterate that the thesis of those commercials is erroneous. The Constitution provides for the pursuit of happiness. We must never put a limit on that pursuit. The Guaranteed Enrollment and Reimbursement Management program will ensure that."

Ott returned to his seat. The Chaplain began to rise to end the service, but before he could reach a standing position, Brandt already was on his feet and at the lectern.

"Of course I had no hand in the placement of that advertisement, and as far as I know, no one directly involved in my campaign has any connection to that particular 501 (c)(4) organization," Brandt said. "Yet I must point out that the Senator's GERM program does include limits on the amount of money that can be spent on each patient in the case of injury during mirth. And I must add, Senator, that the Constitution does not provide for the pursuit of happiness. That would be the Declaration of Independence. I'm not sure we should elect a president who doesn't know the difference."

Brandt began to return to his seat when Ott stood and headed to the lectern. There, both men stood, Ott at the microphone and Brandt menacingly next to him.

"I misspoke, Governor, and I apologize," Ott said. "Sometimes my great patriotism causes my love of all of the sacred documents and texts that serve as the foundation of our government to blur together. For instance, just last week, I was speaking to President Almazbek Atambayev of Kyrgyzstan about our Bill of Rights ..."

"You were not!" Brandt retorted.

"Of course I was!" Ott insisted defensively. "And not just the big amendments, either. Five through ten!"

"I meant you were not talking to Atambayev."

"Was too."

"Well, what does he sound like?"

"What does he sound like? He sounds like the President of Kyrgyzstan."

"What language was he speaking?"

"Kyrgyzstani?"

"Lucky guess."

"I don't need luck," Ott said.

Brandt chortled. "Right," the Governor said. "And I suppose it wasn't luck that the Cubs won Game 5 and that clumsy doofus couldn't make that catch." He quickly turned to the family of the deceased. "No offense," he said.

Buster's mother, stunned by the spectacle, said: "None taken."

"Maybe that was luck," Ott said. "Or maybe it was Providence. Maybe it was justice. Or maybe it was just that the Cubs are a better team than the Red Sox and they're going to win these next two games."

The room, filled mostly with New Englanders, groaned uncomfortably. Ott looked back and saw the contingent from the team he was rooting against sitting there.

"No offense," he said.

"You smug liberal prick," Brandt said. "I can't wait for the Sox to finish off your team tomorrow night so I can focus on kicking your ass in Tuesday's election."

"The only thing you'll be kicking on Tuesday is your dog after you call me to concede the election, you heartless fascist. And don't be surprised if I send your call right to voicemail, either, because I'll be too busy at the double celebration we have planned for Grant Park that night to honor both the Cubs and the next President of the United States!"

And with that, Ott stormed out of the chapel, flanked by his phalanx of crazy-eyed advisers and aides and the Secret Service goons. As he walked past the floral displays, he accidentally knocked the large one from the Cubs over and sent it toppling onto the stool that held the beer cup that was home to the ashes of Buster Sinclair. It was the second time in as many days that someone from Chicago had leveled Sinclair with a baseball.

Scott was glad Ott left when he did. By the time the senator reached the door and stepped out into the flashes of the waiting photographers and videographers, Scott was nearing the last available page of his notebook.

Scott knew he'd have to have two conversations after the memorial service, and while he stood mulling which he wanted to have first, his mind was made up for him.

"Hello, Scott. How are you?"

That was it? Almost four years since they had last seen each other, had managed to find separate orbits, and now their planets were crashing into each other and all Felisha could say was: "How are you?" Nothing profound? Nothing she'd been saving up for nearly half a decade? Nothing to rock him back on his heels or make his head spin?

"Fine," Scott said. "You?"

"I can't wait for this thing to be over," she said.

"I know, me too," Scott said. "Oh, wait, you mean the election? I was talking about the World Series."

"That too," Felisha sighed. "Henry is so wrapped up in the Red Sox that he's losing focus on the campaign. I mean, look what happened here today. He turns a funeral into a debate."

"That was a little strange."

"And then Ott can't help but return fire."

Scott nodded. He was there.

"I guess they both figured that they had prepped for a debate, they might as well have one while they were both in the same room. These guys are like guns. You can't load them and then not pull the trigger."

Scott had no reply, verbal or otherwise. Felisha spoke to him as if they had no history, without comprehension of their past together.

"Anyway," Felisha said, looking down at her BlackBerry, "I should get going. He may want to stop by a few other funeral parlors and cemeteries to rattle off his stump speech."

She spun away. Scott noticed that she was put together so tightly, so molded, that the only part of her that flailed during her spin was the belt on her trenchcoat. Her hair, blouse, slacks and the coat itself remained matted down to her body. Not form-fitting in a sexual way that showed her still impressive curves -- although they did, and Scott noticed that too -- but more of a declaration of her organizational skills. She could command her entire wardrobe to turn as a phalanx of a Grecian army.

Scott almost wondered why they had split up to begin with, but it came flooding back before he could finish the internal question.

In truth, there were a lot of issues that led to the divorce. Traveling on a baseball beat can wear down even granite relationships. Two months of spring training each year. Eighty-one road games a season. Phone calls that tugged him away from the table on Thanksgiving Day, away from the tree on Christmas Day, away from the champagne on New Year's Eve. Scott recalled a veteran pulling him aside one day when he was just starting his career and warning him: *If you love your family, you'll never cover baseball.* Scott thought he could beat the system. He couldn't. No one does. The baseball beat is filled with guys who are thrice-divorced and so removed from their kids that Hallmark could make a line of cards just for them -- *Sorry I missed your graduation, kiddo!* Scott was proud that he had managed to be a decent father despite the gravitational pulls of his job. It was his marriage that couldn't take the G-forces.

But it wasn't just Scott. She had her career too, and the few precious moments when Scott was able to be home, able to be a husband, she was inevitably unavailable. The system worked well enough when it was just the two of them. They could be distant and not know any better. When Ryan was born, though, it was just another direction in which to be yanked. Gumby couldn't handle all of that pulling.

Their relationship had been eroding for years. Felisha had fallen into a deep depression after her client lost the mayoral election. It wasn't her fault. What political adviser could compensate for a candidate hitting on a news anchor during a debate? She didn't feel responsible. She realized she could not have prevented such idiocy, but still.

"I hate losing," she'd said. "Even if it's with a candidate I wouldn't vote for."

In Scott's mind, their marriage ended on the night before his 40th birthday. It was a rare night that the two were in bed together and they were talking about their life, how much of a struggle it had become, but how it was, ultimately, worth the difficulties. Felisha was just coming out of the rut of the mayoral defeat. He'd been patient, allowing her to grieve the professional setback. This was the first deep, heartfelt conversation they'd had in some time.

Scott was glad for it. And anxious for the physical payoff that also had been absent from their lives for some time. He kept glancing at the clock, watching the precious last minutes of his thirties slip away.

When a man turns 40, there are things he needs to prove to himself. To his woman. Scott was at the age at which, thanks to a slew of television commercials, every time he yawned, he had to ask himself: *Is it Low-T?*

At midnight, Scott reached over and gave a familiar tug on the waistband of his wife's panties.

No response. She was asleep. Just a minute ago she was awake and chatting. Now she was out cold. She couldn't even stay awake long enough to welcome Scott into his fifth decade.

Scott had spent many birthdays by himself. That's part of the job. But he'd never felt as alone as he did lying next to his comatose wife and slipping into middle age without so much as a Happy Birthday wish. He thought about giving a stronger tug, but was too angry for that. He considered taking that long walk down the hallway to the bathroom to take care of things himself, but the idea of celebrating one's birthday that way seemed too -- sad. So he rolled onto his back and stared at the ceiling in the midst of a full-blown, middle-of-the-night midlife crisis. For two hours he steamed silently, unflinchingly, over a roiling boil of anger and self-pity, with an occasional flare-up each time she snored.

Finally he made up his mind. It was over. That next evening, Scott huffed out the candles on his cake.

"What'd you wish for?" she asked.

The answer blindsided her.

CHAPTER SEVEN

One of the things that always amazed Scott about baseball was how routinely things happened for the first time. After all those years, a century and a half of record-keeping, you still could show up at a ballpark and get to see something that had never before occurred. Scott loved when word would trickle out through the Internet that someone had hit the first extra-inning grand slam that tied the score and extended a game in Cleveland, or a rookie had posted more stolen bases at the start of his career without getting caught than anyone else ever had. Ever. Even the seemingly silly firsts gave him a thrill. He loved when, in 2002, for instance, opposing starting pitchers in the same game in Cincinnati both were celebrating their birthdays. Believe it or not, that had never happened before.

What really charged Scott was that no one ever seemed to know that these things had never been done ... until they were. There is no empty spot in the record book just waiting for the first player to hit two homers in each game of a doubleheader off the same pitcher. And then, all of a sudden, as if by surprise, it takes place.

Baseball is full of surprises that way.

It also was what Scott liked about Fig. For a while, at least.

Scott had heard it said that living in New York City was like dating a nymphomaniac: For the first six months, you think you're the luckiest son of a bitch who ever lived, but after that, it just becomes exhausting. Living with Fig was that way too. Their relationship lasted longer than six months, but it was a non-stop ride of drinking and getting high and doing stupid things. Bad things. Things college students are supposed to do. Things college graduates are not. Fig never made that transition into adulthood.

The day Scott met Fig, he should have known what he was in for. Scott had moved into the freshman dorm room -- he was the first one there, so he claimed the left side -- and was just hanging up his Roger Clemens poster on the wall when Fig entered and slammed the door behind him, looking around with manic intensity.

Scott introduced himself. Fig ignored him. He flopped on the floor and squirmed under the unmade bed that Scott had not chosen. Fig came back with a large duffel bag. Scott didn't know it was there. He didn't even know Fig had been there.

Fig sprung to his feet, slung the bag over his shoulder, then darted from the room. The door slammed again. Then it opened.

"You coming?"

Scott wasn't sure. He looked at The Rocket on the wall for some guidance. Rocket said nothing, so he followed.

Fig led him to a nearby park. Scott `followed his lead and Fig crouched behind shrubs, Navy SEALed across the lawn, and finally reached a location behind a large tree.

"What are we doing?" Scott asked.

"Shhh!"

"OK," Scott whispered, looking around at the other students who were walking through the park. It was broad daylight. "What are we doing?"

"Take these," Fig said, yanking a pair of military-style binoculars from the bag. "Look over there."

Scott played along.

"What do you see?"

"Some guys playing Frisbee. A couple of girls walking by. A guy and a girl on a bench."

"There, that," Fig said. "Keep your eyes on them."

Fig dug deeper into the duffel and this time came up with two long metal spikes and a sledgehammer. He began nailing the spikes into the ground, speaking between the grunts while he struck them.

"They come here ... every Wednesday ... it's their ... quality time ... are they still ... on the bench?"

"Yes," Scott said, still whispering as much out of shock as in accordance with Fig's earlier demand.

"Is he kissing ... the back of ... her neck?"

"Yes."

"Good," Fig said as he put the sledgehammer down. "I hate when he does that."

Fig then pulled a stretch of rubber tubing from the duffel bag and attached each end to a spike to form a slingshot.

"What are you doing?" Scott asked, still in the whisper.

"Just having a little fun."

With that, Fig reached back into the sack and pulled out a large condom that was filled with a red substance and tied off at the open end.

"What's that?"

"It's a mixture of baby oil, Kool-Aid and about a teaspoon of sperm."

"That's disgusting."

"I didn't want to waste an unused one. Here, put this on."

Fig had more surprises in his duffel bag. He pulled two over-sized steel combat helmets out and handed one to Scott while he placed the other askew atop his own head.

"Just in case they return fire," Fig said. "Now get down and be my spotter."

Scott lay prone on the grass and focused in on the canoodling couple. Fig loaded the condom into the tubing, pulled it back, and released. The condom flew through the air, the liquids inside forcing it to wobble as it made its way across the public space relatively unnoticed. Then, with a gigantic sploosh, it landed. In the parking lot. Just beyond the romantic duo.

"You were about 15 yards long," Scott said.

"Do they suspect anything?"

"Negative."

"Good."

Fig reached back into the duffel and pulled out another loaded prophylactic.

"Is he nibbling her nose?"

"Yes," Scott said.

"Good," Fig said as he hoisted the new condom cannonball into position. "I hate it when he does that."

Fig let the second shot fly. This time it arched high in the air, but it didn't wobble like the first. Scott watched as it sailed true and then landed with a crunching thud on the hood of a red sports car in the parking lot. The car's alarm began to screech, and soon the man who had been getting cozy with his girl was screeching too.

"I've never seen a water balloon dent a car," Scott said.

"That one was filled with cement," Fig said. "Let's go."

On the way back to their dorm, they swam through the fountain in front of their building because Fig said he wanted it to be an amphibious attack. At the other end of the fountain, he stripped out of his clothing so he was naked.

"The enemy can hear the water dripping off your clothes," he warned. He didn't seem to notice -- or care -- that the enemy and the rest of the students could see him clearly and that being bare-assed was not exactly the best camouflage. Scott, who had followed Fig into the water, decided to risk the sounds of the drips.

Finally the two retreated to their dorm room, both of them soaked and out of breath, Fig lying on Scott's bed naked.

"Who was that?" Scott asked as they both panted.

"A girl," Fig said. "And a guy."

"Which were you trying to hit?"

"The guy."

"In order to win …?"

"The girl."

"What's her name?"

Fig said he did not know.

Scott never told Felisha how her first college boyfriend wound up with a dent in the hood of his car.

"She looks great," Fig said as he sneaked up next to Scott to watch Felisha walk away from the Buster Sinclair Memorial Service.

Scott turned and glared at Fig. Fig shrugged.

"She doesn't?"

"What do you want?"

"I don't want anything," Fig said. "I'm just doing my job."

"Let me guess. You're going to have someone hang you upside down by your ankles and slam you into the ballpark so you can write about the demolition from the point of view of the wrecking ball."

"That's not bad," Fig said. "But no."

"So I repeat: What do you want?"

"I told you. Nothing."

The two old friends looked at each other.

"Well, that's not true," Fig said. "I want us to be friends. Or at least friendly."

"Is that why you asked to be put on this assignment?"

Fig's eyes looked hurt.

"I didn't ask for it," he said. "They wanted me to write a few columns off the Series. You know, the final game at the ballpark. The guy in the beer cup over there. The whole thing."

Fig could see the concern in Scott's face.

"You won't even know I'm around," Fig said. "You handle the baseball, I'll take care of the rest of it. It makes both of our lives easier that way."

"You make no one's life easier," Scott said.

"That may be true," Fig said.

"Least of all mine," Scott added.

Fig nodded.

"It's just for a couple of days, Scotty. The Series will be over by the end of the week. Then we can retire to our neutral corners and never see each other again."

"Promise?"

"Have I ever lied to you?"

Even Scott, in his sour mood, had to laugh out loud. Fig appreciated the shared moment. They were the last two at the service.

"Will we ever get past it, Scotty?" Fig asked.

"No," Scott said quickly. "No."

Anyone who has ever played baseball -- or any of the variations of the sport such as softball, kickball, whiffleball, stickball -- knows the feeling. It's a slight twinge in the stomach. A quick gasp from the windpipe. A stiffening of the spine. A physiological reaction when a ball is hit, you instantly calculate the trajectory of it, and you come to the conclusion that it is heading right to you. Even Hall of Fame outfielders who have spent their careers shagging flies effortlessly experience the same rush of readiness when it happens to them. Buster Sinclair likely felt the shudder before his final approach, though he did not live long enough to confirm it. And almost as undoubtedly did Steve Bartman in the 2003 National League Championship Series.

The problem was, Bartman wasn't playing left field for the Cubs that day. He was sitting in Section 4, Row 8, Seat 113 at Wrigley Field when a popup sailed down the third base line and seemed destined to become the 23rd Marlins out of the game, leaving the Cubs with just four more to reach the World Series.

Bartman wasn't the only fan to reach for the rapidly descending sphere as it returned from its pinnacle, where it had momentarily disappeared above the lights. Perhaps Cubs fans had been so used to baseball being a secondary part of the Wrigley experience that they weren't aware enough to not interfere with the game. Perhaps there was such a connection between the team and its fans, both long-suffering, both enjoying the possibilities that lay immediately ahead, that the line between them was blurred.

Whatever the reason, Bartman must have felt that twinge in his gut when the baseball headed his way and never disassociated himself from it long enough to allow the actual left fielder for the Cubs, Moises Alou, to catch the ball. Bartman, in his own attempt to make the catch, knocked the ball away from Alou's mitt and onto the ground.

The Marlins wound up scoring eight runs in that eighth inning, won the game 8-3, and the next day won the pennant and eventually the World Series.

Both the Red Sox and the Cubs had at least one definitive Game Six in their legacy, a contest that was so wrenching and iconic and identifiable that it could be referenced only as "Game Six." The year, the circumstances, the details, they were understood.

For the Cubs, Game Six referred to that 2003 Championship Series against the Marlins. Unmistakably. Singularly.

For the Red Sox, there were two possibilities, and only context could decipher which "Game Six" a Boston fan was talking about. The first was in 1975, when Pudge Fisk clobbered a game-winning homer down the left field line in the World Series against the Reds. Fisk, the burly catcher for the team, used every gram of his body language to pull the ball to the right edge of the left field foul pole and over the big wall. It was one of New England's brightest baseball moments of the century.

The other Game Six was its darkest. After taking a two-run lead in the top of the 10th inning and finding themselves one out away from a World Series title against the Mets, the Red Sox gave up three runs to lose the game, 6-5. The final run was scored by Ray Knight as Mookie Wilson's dribbler down the first base line split the legs of Bill Buckner like a football through the uprights.

Although none of those three Game Sixes eliminated the Cubs or Red Sox from their respective series -- and in fact Fisk's helped keep the team alive -- it should be noted that all three were followed by a loss in Game Seven.

So as Game Six approached at Fenway Park on Halloween Night, on the heels of the snowstorm and the death of the left fielder and the three day layoff, and in the midst of a contentious and unprecedentedly close presidential election that was coming down to its final hours, with both candidates in attendance, the expectation for a dramatic and memorable night was climaxing. Every fan at the park, every player who was in uniform, every reporter in the press box covering the action and every fan at home was experiencing the same feeling that those outfielders and Bartman felt over and over again. *It's coming my way! I got it! I got it!*

Baseball doesn't work that way, though. It does not respond to pressure to live up to expectations. It is only at its most dramatic when drama is least expected.

The Cubs scored four runs in the first inning of Game Six against the Red Sox and cruised to an 11-4 win. No comeback. No memorable home run trots. No "instant classic" status. Just one team easily beating another by seven runs. There were only two baserunners from the sixth inning on. The only thing that stood out from the contest was the fact that the World Series would come down to a deciding Game Seven the following night. And that the season would be over in roughly 24 hours.

It was an easy game for Scott to write. Over in two hours and 56 minutes. All of the action taking place in the first few innings. The narrative simply advancing the following day's game. Scott received just one call from the copy desk, an editor who wanted to clarify whether the single was to right field, as Scott had written, or right-center as it appeared in the wire story that had moved. Scott sighed and explained, as he needed to almost weekly to the night editors, that the almighty Associated Press was not some monolith of journalistic superiority but just the guy who sat three seats away from him and had trouble staying awake during the games. Right, in this case, was right.

The most arduous aspect was lecturing Fig about his calling it "a decisive Game Seven."

"It's the deciding game, not a decisive game," Scott scolded him.

Fig was unimpressed.

"Decisive games are 15-0. Games that determine a championship are deciding games."

Fig shrugged, which only infuriated Scott.

"And another thing. The game isn't tied when it's 3-3. The score is tied. You say 'decisive' and 'tied the game' all the time. Those are things broadcasters say. You're a writer. You should know better. You should be better."

After he filed his final story for the paper, updated a few stats online and tweeted a couple of quotes that had not made it into his copy, he and the other writers he was friendly with headed to their usual watering hole, a place called Magoon's.

Scott began telling Fig stories. On the surface, they were to introduce Fig to the crowd. Deep down, though, Scott was using them as a warning. A red flag. *Caution! Flammable materials!* He did everything but draw a skull and crossbones on Fig.

The stories generally started in one of three ways.

Fig was stoned ...

Fig was drunk off his ...

Fig had just snorted / inhaled / injected ...

From there, Scott tried to find the most embarrassing tales he could recall. It was difficult. So many from which to choose.

There was the time Scott walked into their shared hotel room to find Fig sprawled out naked on the bed, his penis flopping around like an unmanned fire hose while he urinated a rainbow that sprayed every piece of furniture in the room.

There was the time Scott pulled the car over so Fig could puke on the side of the road. He'd managed to open the door but the seatbelt kept him pinned inside the vehicle. When Scott unclipped Fig, he was too inebriated to even put his hands up and he tumbled face-first into the gravel.

There was the time when they were in the Dominican Republic for a story about shortstops and Fig hired a prostitute but spent the next hour pleasuring her. *That's like finding a piece of gum on the sidewalk and putting it in your mouth*, Scott had told him. Fig didn't seem embarrassed in the least by the stories. He even pointed out the scar over his eye from the face-plant on the side of the road.

Scott's maneuver backfired. Not only was he endearing Fig to his baseball-writing buddies, he found himself being charmed by the vulgarity. Especially when Fig began adding the color commentary.

They had the timing of two old friends who could tell a life-time of stories, whose anecdotes could be picked up by either at the turn of a phrase and continued down the path to hilarity. Scott had not forgiven Fig for the incident with Felisha, but he was enjoying their shared recollections. He'd even slipped back into calling him "Figgy."

He reminded himself not to get too close to him, though. While Fig once had claimed to be a descendant of the O'Leary's of Chicago -- the cow lady -- it was never proved except by the constant likelihood of conflagration wherever he went. Bad things happened in his vicinity; that he was, after all, a very bad person. A charming snake who could not be trusted. Manipula-tive, but not in an obvious way. He wouldn't twist your arm, he'd twist your soul. He'd mindfuck you into doing something you never thought you would, something he wanted, and have you believing it was your own idea.

But Scott did enjoy the way he and Fig could play off one an-other. Carl Reiner and Mel Brooks. Only not as old. Or as Jew-ish. And Scott also enjoyed the way the others in the group grav-itated toward their stories. Scott was a good story-teller. Fig was an epic story, though his own narratives were unreliable to the point of ridiculousness. Together the two of them could entertain a bar for hours with tales of their adventures.

"So what happened?" The Professor asked.

"I slept in the lobby," Scott said.

"No, no," The Professor said. "What happened between you two? You were so close. What happened?" The smile left Scott's face, but slowly, a frightened man backing away from a tarantula. He looked at Fig. Scott knew very well what had happened. He wondered if Fig knew it too. If he even remembered. Was it a story they could tell together, passing the narration from one to the other, as they could with many of their escapades? Or was this a Faulkner novel that each of them would tell from a different perspective with differing details, angles and conclusions?

"What happened?" Scott said, repeating the question as its own question. "That's another story."

Scott had enough of his journey to the past with Fig. He turned to head to the bathroom. But when he did, he merged off Memory Lane and found himself heading face-first into traffic on the History Highway. There, walking through the front door with four other well-dressed professionals, was Felisha.

It was 1:47 a.m., Scott noted mentally after a quick glance.

Their terse, cold conversation at the memorial service two days earlier led the rational part of Scott to believe that Felisha's presence at Magoon's was a coincidence. But in a town as full of bars as Boston was, the part of Scott that registered emotions -- pleasure, desire, dread -- felt like Humphrey Bogart in his gin joint. *Of all of them ...*

That Felisha broke away from her pride of politicos and headed straight toward Scott without excusing herself from present company made him even more suspicious. She still was as tightly wrapped in her overcoat and pantsuit as she had been at the farewell to Sinclair that had turned into a presidential debate, at least from the neck down. But her hair was loosened and bounced playfully with each step as she made her way directly for Scott.

Their eyes met and remained focused on each other as Felisha closed the gap between them with purposeful paces. As she drew nearer, though, she showed no signs of slowing her gait. There were no shorter steps in the final few, no easing to a stop. It was as if she were walking toward Scott and intended to walk right through him. And her stare. For a moment, Scott wondered if he was invisible -- not the first time he had felt that way around Felisha -- and if she saw him at all.

Even after their lips met and her right hand swung behind Scott's head, she kept marching forward for two more steps, pushing her taut body against his and forcing him backward the same two paces. Scott could feel how restrictive the jacket and suit corseted her figure, which felt firm and ripe underneath. If she were a peach at a produce stand, he'd have picked her. What he couldn't feel, though, was the passionate public kiss she was putting to him. At least not the way he should have, anyway. There was subtle familiarity in the taste and form, with a dash of new spice to an old recipe that intrigued Scott. but not to the point of arousing anything in him besides curiosity. It was as if he were trying to name that actress from that role in that movie, the one about the thing, and once he was able to with a few quick taps on his phone through the IMDB app, she and her role and her movie would become inconsequential to him.

After several seconds of mostly one-sided reintroduction to each other's palates -- Scott felt himself kiss back at one point, briefly, out of habit, before pulling back -- Felisha disengaged but kept her proximity to Scott so their chest and knees met as she stood on her tippy toes. Scott subconsciously pulled his mid-section back so those parts did not come into contact.

"What are you doing here?" Scott asked as soon as the use of his mouth and all that was encompassed by it belonged to him once again.

"I'm in town with Brandt," she said. Her lips were no longer locked to his, but her eyes were.

"I mean what are you doing here? Here, here?"

For the briefest of flashes, Felisha's visual focus left Scott's face and shifted over his shoulder. It was almost imperceptible, and she returned to his gaze as quickly as she could so as not to further her tell. But Scott knew.

"Fucking Fig," he said.

"I wanted to give you something," she said in a sultry voice that she used when she wanted to receive something, not give it. Felisha was not a giver.

"You just did," Scott said quickly. "Thank you. Very nice. Goodbye now."

"Not that," she said, playfully swatting his shoulder. "This."

She stepped back from Scott, maintaining the almost danger-ous eye contact, just enough to unbuckle her coat and peel the overlapping layers back. Scott could tell how restrictive the belt had been by the slight exhale Felisha gave as she performed the London Fog version of a strip tease. With the flaps of her over-coat pulled back, her form began to regain its figure and Scott couldn't help but think of an infomercial he had recently seen for a memory pillow that returned to its shape even after it had been squished beneath a complete set of the Encyclopedia Britannica. The ad struck him not for the pillow, but because it had been decades since he'd even seen, needed, or thought of an actual encyclopedia.

Felisha then went to work on her navy blue blazer, a three-button job that she popped deliberately, seductively, one by one, each release allowing the hidden cleavage of her white blouse to be exposed more and more. This time it was Scott whose quick glance betrayed him, but by the time he returned to Felisha's stare, she was smiling.

"What are you going to do, get undressed right here in the bar?"

She shook her head from side to side just as the third button came unclasped, then rolled her head around her neck to enjoy the freedom from her restraining wardrobe that had been pinching and grabbing and squeezing all day.

"Not here," she said.

Then she reached inside her freshly unbuttoned suit jacket and pulled out a long white envelope, held it up with a ta-dah flourish, and pressed it against Scott's chest.

"What's this?"

"Open it."

"What is it? I'm not playing games."

Felisha gave a cross-lipped pout, then blinked. It was the first time since she'd entered the bar that Scott noticed her blink.

"A ticket," she said. "To Hawaii. One of three. One way."

"What am I supposed to do with it?"

"Use it."

"Stop talking like that."

"Like what?"

"Like you're Mae Fucking West."

"Still with the similes, Scott?"

Scott was as angry as a, as a, well, so angry he couldn't think of anything at the time.

"What is this?" he asked.

Felisha dropped from her tippy toes and stood flat-flooted in front of Scott.

"I want you to come and live with me. In Hawaii."

"What?"

"I want. You to come. And live with me. In ..."

"I heard you. Why would I do that?"

"Because I want us to be back together, Scott," she said. "I didn't know I did until I saw you at the debate the other day."

"The memorial service," Scott corrected. "For a friend of mine."

"That depends on your perspective," she volleyed with a smirk. "To me it was a debate. And I was so wrapped up in it that when I saw you there, it took a few hours for it to register. It wasn't until I got back in the car with Brandt that I realized how much I wanted you. How much I wanted us."

The conversation paused as Scott, already a bit boozy, tried to process the events.

"Wait, three tickets?" he barked. "You spoke to Ryan about this?"

"No," she said.

"Swear to me."

"I didn't. I know the rules. Besides, I wanted us to do it together."

"He's just gotten over us being apart and now you want to put him through us getting back together? Besides, he loves staying with my folks."

"He loves me, too. I'm his mother."

"What about Brandt?" Scott said, his brain shuffling through the deck of 52 reasons why this was a horrible idea. "What if he wins?"

"He won't win," Felisha said.

"It's close. What if he does? You'd have a spot in the Administration, right?"

"I'm sure I'd be asked."

"But you wouldn't take it?"

"No," she said, then smiled coyly. " 'I've decided to spend more time with my family.' I always wanted to say that."

Scott shook his head in disbelief.

"What about my job?"

"You won't have to work," Felisha said. "The way I've billed on this campaign, we could live four lifetimes in luxury. In paradise."

Scott stood in silence.

"Ryan would be so happy," she cooed. "The waves. The beach … Us."

"Get out of here," Scott said with a new fire. He would not allow Felisha to use Ryan to manipulate him. "Get the fuck out of here."

"OK," Felisha said. "OK. But in one day this baseball season will be over. And in three days this election will be over. And I'll be out of a job."

Scott remembered how miserable their lives together had become. He remembered the betrayal soon after their separation. It wasn't just Felisha who broke his heart that night, it was Fig, too.

"Get out of my head, bitch!" Scott yelled.

Felisha smiled.

"Get out my bar, bitch!" he yelled.

Felisha slowly lifted her frame up on her toes once again and leaned in toward Scott. She was coming for another kiss, but this time, just before their lips met, she was diverted away, swinging to the left and accelerating, a car making a move for the passing lane on a highway. She found his ear.

"Think about it," she whispered, then rolled her tongue under his lobe and subtly reached her hand up to brush against the crotch he had been careful to keep distant from her. It moved, and what's worse, Scott knew that Felisha knew that it moved. Felisha didn't even look back at him as she walked away, her liberated hips and bottom swinging with satisfaction as her overcoat and suit jacket and hair all bounced in perfect rhythm. She slid the overcoat off her shoulders, folded it neatly over her arm, and slid into a booth with the group she had entered Magoon's with. There, waiting for her at the table, was a martini. *Dirty*, Scott thought about the drink she always ordered, insisting on extra brine. She took a sip. Finally she looked back at Scott. And winked.

Dirty, he thought again.

Scott just stood there, steaming. He was pissed off at Felisha for her intrusion back into his life. He was ticked at Fig for whatever role he played in this chance encounter (and he was certain it was not a small one). He was angry at himself for even allowing himself to think about the possibility of what Felisha had proposed, even in the most hypothetical of realms. Why did he have to rattle off reasons not to? Her career? His? What did any of that matter? And Ryan? To bring him into it was demonic. His answer should have been no. Immediately no. Definitively no. No, no, no.

It wasn't until Scott returned home and stood in front of the mirror in his bedroom that he realized he still had the envelope with the tickets in it.

If ever there was a morning when Scott needed a game day run, it was this one. The first day of November. The last day of the season. And so many thoughts banging around in his head, flying in various directions like baseballs in batting practice. The guys on the field for those workouts have large nets and cages and screens to protect them from the wayward projectiles, though. Scott's psyche was fully exposed and taking fire from all angles.

He had thought about throwing away the envelope from Felisha when he realized he'd brought it home just a few hours ago, but he decided that Ryan might find it in the trash. He'd never been one to pay much attention to wastebasket contents, but Scott figured it would be just his luck to have him stumble upon this one. Then he'd have to explain it. And he didn't want to explain it to Ryan. He wasn't even sure he wanted to or could explain it to himself.

So he folded the envelope in half and tucked it into his sock drawer.

While it still was dark, about an hour before his alarm was scheduled to blare the guitar riffs of Aerosmith's "Walk This Way" that he'd chosen as his wake-up song on his iPhone, he rolled out of bed and stuffed the envelope in his work bag. Better to have it close to him, he thought, than out of sight where anyone else could find it.

Out on his run, he felt nervous about leaving the envelope anywhere in the house, even in the satchel Ryan would never in a million years pry into. He should just destroy it. Burn it. It seemed old-fashioned and vindictive and dramatic to actually burn the document. A bit silly, even. After all, it wasn't the paper that could get him onto that plane for paradise but the series of numbers that was printed on it that corresponded to his name. He could easily show up at the airport for the flight with nothing more than his driver's license and have a fresh boarding pass printed for him and meet Felisha at the gate and …

What was he thinking about? Again with the possibilities instead of the certainty of a no.

He quickly changed mental focus to Fig, whom he blamed for the fiasco of the previous night. *Fuckin' Fig!* And now they had to work together. They hadn't said more than 10 words to each other in the past decade, and now they were covering the biggest story of Scott's career together. Whether or not the Red Sox won or lost later that night in the World Series, in Game Seven of the World Series, it would be a story that Scott would be remembered for. Decades from now, when historians looked back on the game that decided the clash between the Cubs and the Sox, they'd be searching for his byline. It was an awesome responsibility when Scott thought about it that way. Which was why he tried not to. Besides, he knew anything he wrote would pale next to whatever Fig came up with. It certainly did last night. While Scott wrote the story of the lackluster Game Six, Fig had spent most of the game watching it on television ... with Bartman.

Scott had been trying to nail down an interview with the elusive fan for years, and felt he was coming close in recent weeks. Then Fig was able to lure the outcast from his den of woe, fly him to Boston, and bring him to a local bar, where the two of them watched the Cubs win in near anonymity. Bartman had had Lasix surgery since he was last seen in public in 2003, so he no longer wore the identifiable glasses. And no one wore turtlenecks anymore. As for the Cubs hat? Well, there were enough of them in the city for him to blend in with his perched atop his head.

It was a hell of a piece. Bartman telling Fig about how this Series could change his existence, how if the Cubs won a championship, he might be able to get on with his life and no longer be the most hated man in Chicago. Spilling his guts about what he was thinking as the ball sailed toward him on that fateful night when he was transformed from a fan with the best seat in the house to a pariah; how he had to change his address and his parents had to move out of their home of 48 years and his sister had to drop out of Northwestern; the intricacies, near-misses and pitfalls of staying out of the public eye for as long as he had. It was glowing stuff, particularly the end, when a Cubs fan in the bar finally recognized Bartman. And bought him a drink.

"How does he get stories like that?" The Professor asked Scott.

"You ever see graffiti on an overpass or high on a building and wonder how the hell someone got up there to make it? Wonder what kind of person would risk a deadly fall just to make his mark?"

"Yeah," The Professor said.

Scott nodded.

"Me too."

Scott hated Fig, but he had to tip his cap to his work. He despised working with him, but he was glad to have him on his side, in his paper, and not have to wake up in disgust each day wondering how he'd been beaten this time. At least now when Scott woke up in disgust over Fig, it had nothing to do with journalistic competition.

Fig hadn't even said a word about the Bartman interview or story at the bar the night before. Scott wished he had been as discreet with Felisha. Why he would stick his nose in Scott's personal life after all this time was something that Scott could not figure out. At least not yet.

Scott thought about Ryan. He seemed happy. Could he be happier in Hawaii? Scott thought about Buster Sinclair. He thought about Darryl Hoyt, the starting pitcher for the Sox in Game Seven. What must he be doing this morning? He thought about Brandt and Ott. He still had no idea whom he would be voting for the following day.

It was a Monday morning. The streets were still littered with candy wrappers, egg shells and shaving cream from the previous night's Halloween festivities, and the parochial school that Scott often ran past -- St. Angus -- was closed for All Saints Day. It was a day to honor and remember the dead.

Scott ran his usual route toward the ballpark, enjoying the crispness of the cold air that he much preferred to the humid and thick air that sublet the space in the summer. There had been talk of snow that day -- Snow! Again with the snow! -- but the storm had moved out to the Atlantic, and while it was frigid this morning, the temperatures were expected to reach the 40s by the afternoon. There was no meteorological issue that would force a postponement of this game, as had happened in Chicago.

He made his way up Brookline, hung a right on Boylston, cut down Yawkey Way and hooked back around Brookline to the front of the park. There, as he made the turn, he was stopped cold by a sawhorse with yellow flashing lights. Probably a safety precaution, he figured, as he tried to keep his legs moving while catching his breath and figuring out how to continue his path around the stadium. This was where the heavy machinery for the demolition had been parked throughout the season. It was where the guys in the blue hats gathered and where the wrecking ball-slash-tourist attraction hung ominously for the last few months.

Only Scott didn't see the familiar wrecking ball. It was gone. Most of the other machines and trucks and heavy equipment were still in place, but the ball itself was missing. Scott was wondering where it might have gone when the piercing sound of an airhorn blaring was so jarring, he had to put his hands over his ears to protect them from the high-pitched screech. And then, from the corner of his left eye, he saw the ball.

Ted Williams used to say he could see the stitches on a baseball that was pitched to him, could see the way they spun and interacted with each other, and immediately determine what kind of pitch it was, where it would end up, and whether or not it

would be a strike worth swinging at. Scott saw the stitches on the
wrecking ball now, painted in bright red against the white face of
the steel sphere, but they weren't spinning. A knuckleball. But
not darting and wiggling either. This was moving like a fastball
for sure.

Right down the middle.

With the velocity and force of a train locomotive and the
whoosh of a fighter jet, the ball swung taut on its cable, from
Scott's left to his right, and met the face of Fenway Park, where
it found little resistance. Bricks bounced off it, wood splintered
from it, sparks flew from the wires severed by it. The rumble of
the collision could be felt through the sidewalk where Scott
stood, still jogging in place.

So shocked was he by what he saw, he didn't even notice the time.

PART TWO

CHAPTER EIGHT

Szczesny destroyed for a living. And he enjoyed it.

It made him feel powerful to sit in his chair, high above the people in the street, an elevated lord, pulling the levers that made the large machine lurch and spin and gobble up buildings. With the slide of his wrist, he was able to swing the 20,000-pound iron ball as if it were a yo-yo, smashing it into walls and through windows, then pulling it back up again, under control, only to take another swipe.

He'd come to America to create. He wanted to build. He wanted to shape. He wanted to make an imprint on the great country that his father had always told him about. Instead, he was tearing it down, razing it one crash at a time.

At first it troubled him. Who was he to wield such force, such authority? He'd been in the country for less than a year and was now demolishing buildings that had been standing in place for more than a century. It was difficult to come to grips with the finality of it all.

He thought of the workers -- immigrants like himself, no doubt -- who had gotten up early in the morning and made their way to a worksite just as he did, only decades earlier. They lifted the bricks, slathered them with mud, placed them in their proper spot by hand. They riveted the steel, nailed the wood. They built. Then, in the span of a lucky man's lifetime, Szczesny came along and smashed it to piles of rubble. He didn't even have the decency to do it by hand, the way the buildings went up. He simply ordered the machine to do it and the iron ball was at his bidding. What took men weeks or months to mold through callous and blister, costing them their backs and fingers, neither of which would ever again be close to as straight as the red and brown rows of bricks that they planted, Szczesny flattened in a morning.

Eventually, though, he found beauty in the destruction. Like a mortician who takes pride in his ghastly work, Szczesny blocked out the idea of death, the thought that the walls would never be again, and focused on the necessity of his labor. He may not have been building, but he was clearing the way for those who would. He was a prophet of progress, delivering his message that change was coming and believing all the while that it was change for the better. He even prayed for the buildings before striking them down.

It made it easier for him if he paid attention to the details. Instead of aiming his wrecking ball at a wall, he'd focus it on a single brick. What must have seemed chaos and rampage and muddled measure, he turned into surgical strikes and personal touches. A hunter, he appreciated the sportsmanship of a quick kill. Glancing blows were unfair to the buildings. The fewer swings it took, the better. He dispatched with dignity, not disarray.

He was working for Barcikowski & Marecki International -- BMI -- when he awoke on the first day of November and felt the sharp whip of Boston cold snap him on the tip of his nose.

The puff of white air rose like the first morning coughs of a diesel engine, a sight so familiar to Szczesny that it took him several bleary blinks to realize it emanated from his own mouth and not a machine. The biting chill grabbed onto the tip of his crooked nose like one of the pit bulls he often saw walking around the neighborhood and shook him to consciousness. Awake. Frigid. But awake.

He'd slept in his parka with the hood pulled up over his ears that night. There was no heat in the apartment and the few blankets he did own were lazy workers, more decorative than useful. Still on his back, still wrapped in his parka with the fur-lined hood framing another puff of white air rising toward the ceiling, visible only for the first few inches before fading into the early morning abyss, Szczesny started looking around the dark room for familiarity. He'd been in the place for only three nights, ever since his move to Boston from New York, when BMI sent him up I-95 because extra workers were needed. That wasn't long enough for him to form any kind of relationship with the edges, corners and shapes that surrounded him. He couldn't even remember at first which side of the bed the lamp was on, the lamp he'd gotten from his aunt and uncle, two people with whom he was as unfamiliar as his surroundings. Since arriving, he'd been groping through life in a cryptic room; hands outstretched, looking for a switch, a wall, the hollowness of a door, while at the same time bracing for a collision.

He sat up and reached to his right, grabbing through the darkness, until he brushed against the vinyl shade that topped the green glass base and felt its ripples. He slid his fingers down the shade then up and under, feeling his way for the knob to turn the light on. With a click, all the unknowns should have become illuminated. He looked around. The lamp did little. They still were unknowns, obscured even more by the frozen cloudiness of every breath he exhaled.

Szczesny had been cold in Poland. There were dark mornings in Warsaw when he did not want to get out of bed. There, at least, he had his blankets for warmth. He knew where the lamp was. Here, in America, in Boston, the cold pierced him more deeply, as if uncertainty had a wind chill factor. Slowly he swung his legs from the bed and stood up. He took off the parka, if only to give himself the illusion of being fresh when he would put it on again in 20 minutes to head out. It was so cold that the water in the toilet had frozen on top and he had to poke through the ice with his finger so he could urinate.

Uncle Zid, his father's brother who had come to America when he was six, had gotten him the job with BMI. Uncle Zid knew Marecki from the Polish American Citizens Club, a once vibrant organization that was now dying of old age. Where hundreds used to gather weekly to eat, dance and speak the old language, now only a few dozen gathered every other month. Zid -- the name was shortened and somewhat Americanized from Zdzislaw -- was the youngest member of the club. He was 58. It had been so long since they'd admitted any new members, no one could even remember how to do it when Zid suggested that his nephew join.

Zid could speak only some Polish, having spent his life trying to acclimate to his surroundings in America. Szczesny spoke no English. To communicate, they had to have Jan Kozak, a woman from the club who taught the neighborhood children the culture, customs and language of Poland, act as an intermediary.

But neither Zid nor Jan was around the previous night to translate the voicemail that was left at Szczesny's number.

"Hey, Shhhh-shhhh-chzzz-ny, I guess it is," the messenger said, spitting and shushing through Szczesny's name like a zealous librarian. "Anyway, this is Lou at BMI. The foreman on the

Fenway job. Sorry to call so late, I had to take the kids out for tricks or treats and then was watching the game. Obviously, we're going to have to delay the demo for the Series. I know we were scheduled to tear the sucker down tomorrow, but, well, they couldn't fucking close out the Cubs like they should have. Can Murphy get a hit in this series, for Christ's sake? Anyway, we'll reschedule the demo for sometime soon, probably next week after the parade when the Sox win. So, um, yeah. That's it. We'll be in touch tomorrow late morning and let you know where to report to. I'm sure something needs to be taken down. Go Sox!"

Szczesny had sat on his cot the night before, unable to speak enough English to even dare answering the phone, staring at the machine as he heard the message come through it. He did not even recognize his own name, so badly had Lou butchered it. The only words he recognized were "BMI" (which was his employer), "Fenway" (which was the job he was scheduled to do the following morning) and the last word, "*sauks,*" which he recognized as Latvian (he'd learned a few phrases in that language from a neighbor back in Poland and knew that *sauks* meant "will be called"). He had no idea why someone would break into Latvian at the end of an English message, but he eagerly anticipated the next call.

When it didn't come, he just got up and went to work.

Even as he stopped by the newsstand on his way to the job that morning, Szczesny had no way of knowing what the English papers were screaming at him about the game that was to be played that night. He read only the Polish-language papers, and they had nothing in them about baseball.

So, at 7:45 a.m. on Monday morning, November 1, Szczesny was where he believed he was supposed to be: sitting at the controls of the wrecking ball that was destined to tear down the old sports facility in front of him. He hardly noticed that no other workers were around, as it was fairly common for the Americans to show up at the last minute and his was really just a one-man job. It wasn't until he was done swinging his 10-ton yoyo that another crew could come in with trucks and load the rubbish for removal.

Szczesny set up the area as he often had, placing warning sawhorses to keep pedestrians at bay. He even nodded to a police officer when he placed one of the detours at the corner of Landsdowne and Brookline. Those in the neighborhood were so used to seeing the blue construction hats in the area that the cop actually helped Szczesny set up his barricade.

At 9 a.m., just as a jogger was coming around the corner, Szczesny pulled the lever to bring the ball into position, sounded his air horn as a warning, scanned the area visually to make sure no one was in any danger, and let 'er fly.

This time it was Scott calling JKL. To see if he had gotten the email. About the text.

Come on, come on, pick up the phone.

"You're up early," JKL said when he finally answered.

"It's gone!" Scott shouted.

"What's gone?"

"Fenway!"

"How can it be gone? What do you mean, gone?"

"What do I mean? I mean a wrecking ball just ploughed through it! I'm standing here on the street outside and looking straight in at the infield grass!"

"How could ..."

"I don't know!"

"Wow," JKL said with a gasping whisper, bringing calm to the situation. "OK."

"Yeah," Scott said, following his editor's lead. "Wow."

"Do you have any pictures?"

Pictures! Scott thought. Dammit, how could he not think to take pictures!

"No. Not yet."

"Take a few and then email them to me."

"You don't believe me?"

"For the website. Once they close this down as a crime scene, we won't be able to get our photographers in there."

"Crime scene?"

"It's a terrorist act, Scott. They'll push everyone and everything back to a perimeter. Just like they did with the Marathon."

Scott hadn't thought of the possibility that the destruction of the stadium could be linked to some international terrorism. Jihadists were not known to be fond of using wrecking balls to employ their destruction. But as wave after wave of Boston Police cruisers made their way to Fenway and began cordoning off the area, it became clear to Scott that he might in fact be at the newest Ground Zero of the latest attack on America.

"OK," Scott said, suddenly unnerved by the police presence, looking over his shoulder and thinking about some other piece of heavy machinery suddenly coming to life and throwing haymakers at the stadium. He hung up on JKL and switched his iPhone over to camera mode. He clicked away at the hole in Fenway Park, at the crowd of people who were now surrounding it. He snapped pictures of dazed delivery men and curious grounds crew members who came walking out of the stadium, stepping over the piles of rubbled bricks and making their way through the newly, crudely established front door. He captured the police officers pushing everyone back away from the ballpark, just as JKL said they would be doing.

Scott did not feel safe, though, until he turned the camera toward the control booth for the wrecking ball. There, as he zoomed in with his fingers on the screen, he was able to see the face of the man who had launched the ball that went through Fenway. He was just sitting there, stunned, watching as combat-armed SWAT officers surrounded him. He seemed as surprised to see them as Scott was when he saw the wrecking ball in flight. Slowly, the man at the controls put his hands up in the air. Had this been an act of violence or meant to carry a message -- political or otherwise – Scott decided that the perpetrator certainly would have expected to be met with such a show of force. Planned on it, even. This guy was shocked by the attention he was receiving.

Scott continued to click away. But he knew that the man who had launched the attack was no terrorist.

TERRORIST!!!

That was the headline screaming on the paper's website just a few moments after Scott emailed the pictures to JKL.

Exclusive photo of the man behind the plot to destroy Fenway Park!

Big type. Lots of exclamation points. This was serious.

Underneath the picture and its headline were a few paragraphs that Scott had cobbled together with his trembling thumbs on his phone and sent in. It was a basic outline of what had happened. The who, what, where, when, etc. At approximately 9 o'clock, on Monday November 1, the morning of Game Seven of the World Series, the wrecking ball hit the front of Fenway Park. There did not appear to be any injuries or fatalities. Police were closing off the area. There was one man in police custody. As Scott was hurried away from the scene, he read the story in his palm. He noticed a few typos. He wrote Fenway "Fenawy." And the copy used the phrase "9 a.m. this morning" which any copy editor would have caught as redundant. That's how quickly the desk had to get the story online. There was no time to polish the silverware.

Nowhere in the copy did Scott refer to the situation as a terrorist act, or even a criminal one. He made no mention of there being a plot. And yet there was his byline (and photo credit) right under the blaring word and damning subhead that were sure to catch the world's attention.

CHAPTER NINE

Felisha was just about to knock on the door to the hotel suite when the ding of the elevator at the end of the hallway caught her attention. This was supposed to be a private floor, with guests needing a special key to reach it. The elevator should not have been stopping here. Cleaning crews and other hotel employees were supposed to use the service elevator at the other end of the building. Her curiosity was piqued as the doors rolled open. *Who would it be?* she wondered. *A journalist looking for a scoop? A wayward tourist? Scott?*

She never considered the possibility that it would be six federal agents with their guns drawn, running at her full speed and screaming at her to get down on the ground and away from the door. Felisha didn't have time to process those orders before she found herself pancaked by one of the agents, tackled to the hallway carpet, her cheek rubbing against the gaudy amoebas that created its pattern.

"STAY DOWN! STAY DOWN!" the agent demanded of her, his firearm pointing not directly at her head so as to be too threatening but in the general vicinity of it so that it was nearby if needed. Felisha had no choice. She felt as if she were going to die.

She heard the other agents communicating on the radio attached to the shoulder of the man who was Panini-pressing her.

Who is she?

Can we get an ID here?

Felisha tried to answer the questions herself, but the weight of the agent on top of her plus the force of the fall to the floor had squeezed almost all of the air from her body. She was a deflated accordion trying to wheeze out a single note, pressing all of the keys but producing no sound.

She could see and hear, though.

"Secure!" the agent on top of her stated matter-of-factly.

"Going in!" another said, and with swift efficiency, he kicked open the door to the suite that Felisha had just a moment ago been ready to politely tap to get the Governor's attention. The heavy door crashed open and banged against the inside wall with such force that it swung back around toward the jamb and nearly closed all the way again. Before it could, though, the remaining five agents pushed their way past it and scrambled throughout the suite.

Felisha still was pinned to the floor, but she could raise her head enough to see some of what was happening inside the suite. Her captor remained in place, his gun just a quick flinch from her head.

"Clear!" one of the agents from inside yelled. "No Bruin!"

"No Bruin here!" another yelled.

Felisha began piecing together what was happening. Bruin was the Secret Service code name for Brandt. They called him that because he had been a political science professor at UCLA, but Brandt didn't mind the handle because he always thought it made him sound like a hockey player for his favorite Boston team.

"Clear!" another agent yelled. "Where is he?"

"I have Bruin!" came a holler from what seemed to be the farthest reaches of the suite. "I have Bruin. He's in the shower."

Felisha could hear Brandt yelling back but could not quite make out his words. Other than to recognize about every other one as a profanity.

"Sir, we have to leave," the agent said calmly but clearly and loudly. "Now!"

"What's happening?" Brandt asked. "Why?"

"Now, sir!" the agent replied.

"Can I at least put on some clothes?"

"No."

"A towel?"

"Here," the agent said. "Take this. Now let's move."

Two agents filed out the door past Felisha, and she noticed the second of them had his bulletproof vest exposed. All the rest wore their standard issue navy blue windbreakers with yellow letters on the front chest and larger ones across the back.

Then, behind him, came a third agent hustling a nearly naked Brandt out of the room. Still dripping wet from the shower, the only thing Brandt wore was a navy blue windbreaker tied around his waist so that the body of the jacket aproned his front while the sleeves of the garment tangled together behind him. The nylon made it hard for the sleeves to stay together, and Brandt fumbled to keep them engaged with each other as he was ushered into the hallway. The agents led him in the direction opposite from where they had entered, heading for the service elevator.

Brandt did not make eye contact with Felisha as he stepped over her in the hallway, but Felisha had the misfortune of looking straight up as he strode above her, the jacket flailing in the wind of activity like the kilt of a fierce Scottish warrior. The agent remained on top of Felisha as the rest of the crew filed past. Just before he turned the corner for the elevator, though, Brandt yelled out: "She's with me! She's good!"

One of the agents trailing the Brandt Express turned back and gave a thumbs-up to the one on top of Felisha.

"You're good," he told her.

Then he grabbed the front of Felisha's suit and stood up so that he brought Felisha to her feet with him. He kept a tight grip on her as they brought up the rear of the caravan.

At first Felisha thought it might be so she wouldn't take off, as if she were in custody. Then she quickly realized that she didn't have the strength to go anywhere and that the agent's grip actually was the only thing keeping her upright, his movement the only thing propelling her forward, allowing her to keep up with whatever it was they were doing.

They made good time and caught up to the group in front of them, closing in on Brandt's bare ass as it jiggled beneath two tails of blue nylon. By the time they reached the end of the hall-way, Felisha and her ride had pulled even.

They reached the elevator doors just as they dinged and slid open. Two more agents were inside waiting. The two new agents stepped out while the first six and the new members of their entourage -- Felisha and Brandt -- crammed into the box. Someone hit "LR" on the buttons, sending them down to the lobby level where they would exit through the rear of the car.

Brandt finally had time to properly tie the sleeves behind him, crisscrossing them twice so they remained in place but still exposed his wet buttocks that were leaving a puddle on the floor of the elevator.

"Where are we going?" Felisha asked in a whisper, though not a purposeful one. She still was only half inflated and trying desperately to inhale as much oxygen as she could with each deep breath.

The elevator hit the lobby level and the rear doors opened into the hotel kitchen. Brandt was led out first, escorted through

the startled staff that was busy filling room service breakfast orders. Grease from a large tray of bacon leaped in the air and
singed Brandt on the butt as he passed it. Then Felisha and her
escort followed.

"Where are we going?" she asked again, this time in a somewhat fuller tone. She knew she had been heard. And yet she received no answer.

Emerson Ott stood up.

"You gotta be shitting me," he said.

The senator from Illinois and presidential candidate looked
around the windowless storage room with big round banquet tables on their sides, their legs folded inside of them and crossed,
and stacks of chairs covered in red fabric and lined up in piles of
10. He'd been in the room for 20 minutes, but it was only 10
minutes earlier that he'd stopped pacing long enough to consider
taking one of those chairs off the top and using it. Two of his
aides leaned against a wall where they had cleared away some
crates of recently laundered cloth tablecloths and napkins, whispering what little updates they could scrounge to each other as
they checked their BlackBerries.

But Ott sat in the middle of the room, tapping his foot impatiently, until the door opened and he thought for a moment it was
time to leave. That's why he stood.

Only this wasn't an escape. He hadn't made bail. The judge had
not found leniency. They were putting two more prisoners in the cell.

"You have got to be fucking shitting me," he repeated with
more enunciation. "I can't even get my own secure undisclosed
location?"

The agents said nothing as they ushered -- pushed -- Governor Brandt and Felisha into the storage room. Now there were

five of them in the small space. Two of them were running for president. The next day. On their way to the storeroom, Brandt's party had passed a lost-and-found box. The agents graciously gathered a pair of gray sweatpants that were too large and a Celtics T-shirt that was too small for Brandt to wear after he was removed from the threatening situation nearly nude. Ott was in a suit and tie, or had been. The jacket was now hanging over a chafing rack next to the door and the tie was nearly unknotted, loosened and tugged at with so much frustration and anxiety that the knob where the two ends of fabric met hung low. It looked more like a sash than neckwear.

The two teams just stood there for a moment, each unsure exactly what was going on but unwilling to flash their ignorance. Brandt and Felisha glanced around the room to get a feel for the surroundings and quickly realized that their roommates had been there for a considerable amount of time. They'd already established it as a camp, moving the furniture of the room around to fit their needs.

Felisha broke the silence.

"Signal?" she asked the opposing aides, holding up her BlackBerry.

They looked at each other, unsure whether to forfeit their information. Since they had none to forfeit, they answered truthfully.

"Hardly," the younger of the two said. "I think we're in a basement."

"We came in at street level and the elevator went down at least two floors," Felisha said with a nod. "Any idea what's happening up there?"

"Not exactly," the older aide said. "Some kind of international threat in the city, from what I can piece together. They're mobilizing troops toward Poland."

"Poland?" Felisha asked.

"That's all we have," the older one said curtly, trying to give off an air of holding out even though he wasn't.

"What do you know?" the younger one asked.

"Just the threat part," Felisha said, shaking her BlackBerry as if that would reset it, as if it were a thermometer, as if the movement would allow her to capture a stronger signal to the rest of the world. "We didn't know about Poland," she added.

"What were you doing, playing pickup with Tawmmy and Sully?" Ott asked Brandt in a harsh fake Boston accent.

"We left in a rush," Felisha answered for her boss as he rolled his shoulders uncomfortably in the Kelly green T-shirt that was two sizes too small and, even more offensive to him, had on the back the name and number of Paul Pierce, who had not played for the Cs in several years.

"Yeah," Ott said. "Well, I hope you're not in a rush anymore."

"Have they told you how long?"

"No," the younger aide told Felisha. "They haven't told us anything."

Silence. Staring.

"You weren't here?" the older aide asked. "When they grabbed you?"

"No," Felisha said. "We were at the Four Seasons."

Then Felisha realized she didn't even know where "here" was. So she asked.

"The Sheraton," the younger aide said. "We were here. Just about to leave to fly to Milwaukee and then Columbus. And then ..."

"Yeah," Felisha said with understanding. "And then."

Another moment of silence.

"Portland," she said. "That's where we were going."

"Maine or Oregon?"

"Maine," Felisha said. "We wanted to stay relatively local. For tonight."

Everyone nodded. Of course. Game Seven.

"Well," Felisha said with a sigh after yet another awkward moment of silence. "I guess we'd better get comfortable."

"Christ," Brandt said, glancing at his naked wrist for where his watch would have been, "they'd better let us out of here before the game starts."

CHAPTER TEN

Scott received the terse email from Sy Galoosh that was CC'd to
every other baseball writer who was in town to cover the game.
Press conference. 1 p.m. Boston Hyatt.
Moments later he received a second message that was just for him.
Can you come at noon?
Yes, Scott wrote back. *See you there.*
An hour later, Scott walked in through the lobby of the hotel.
He wasn't surprised to see such a heavy police presence. The
city and the world still were acting under the premise that Boston
had been attacked by a Polish terrorist, in part thanks to his
newspaper's website, which had run his story and his photograph, both with his byline. Scott couldn't help but feel a sense
of responsibility over the frenzy, even though, as he kept remind-
ing himself, he'd written nothing to indicate that the incident was
nefarious in any way.

A heavily-armed officer checked his photo identification.
Scott walked toward the hotel bar, where he saw Sy Galoosh
leaning against a pillar scanning his phone. Galoosh must have
felt Scott's presence because he looked up and caught his stare
and the two walked toward each other.

"Thanks for coming, Scott," Galoosh said.

"No problem," Scott said with an absurd stress on the banality of their conversation, as if they were meeting for ice cream on a summer evening. "I wasn't doing anything."

"Scott, let me take you upstairs."

The rode together in the elevator silently, each checking his phone for updates from CNN, Fox, NBC News, TMZ, ESPN, and any other news-gathering outlet that was trying to play catch-up to Scott's exclusive. So far his were the only photographs of the terrorist (as he was presumed to be) and the damage he'd inflicted on America's favorite ballpark just hours before it was about to take its final bow.

"Anything?" Galoosh asked.

"Not much," Scott said. "I don't think it's terrorism, though."

"Uh-huh," Galoosh said.

They stepped out of the elevator car, turned a corner, walked down the hallway past four doors and stopped in front of room 1427. Galoosh patted his pockets until he found the credit card-looking plastic key and the two of them entered. The Commissioner was standing in front of the window, hands folded behind him, looking out in the distance.

"Sir," Galoosh said, clearing his throat to get The Commissioner's attention. "Sir, Scott Findle is here. Sir?"

"Yes!" he said as he turned around startled, a man who suddenly had no idea how long he'd been staring at nothing. "Yes, Scott. Thanks for coming. Thanks for your help."

"You're welcome," he said reflexively before his reporter's suspicion was aroused. "Help with what?"

"Scott," Galoosh said, "we have to make a decision on what to do. We have a press conference in an hour and we have no information. The police, the mayor, BosCAM, even the feds in D.C., they're all in the dark. No one can tell us what kind of damage we're looking at, how long it may take to fix it, nothing.

And they certainly won't allow us to go down to the ballpark and take a look at it ourselves."

Scott nodded.

"We need some intel, young man," The Commissioner said, walking up to Scott and patting him on the shoulder. "You're the only one who has been to the scene and come back. The only one we know of, anyway. We need to know what we're dealing with so we know how to deal with it."

The Commissioner smiled peacefully. Blithely.

"Well," Scott said, "what do you want to know?"

"Can it be fixed?"

"I'm not an engineer," Scott said.

"I understand that. But you're a rational person. A reporter. An observer and an analyzer. Can it be fixed?"

"Eventually, I guess," Scott said. "Not by tonight."

"Was there any structural damage?"

"Well, yeah," Scott said. "There's a hole in it."

"I mean did it look as if it might collapse? Would there be a danger to fans?"

"I don't … I mean … I would think …"

Scott didn't know how to answer.

"Why don't you just describe what it looks like," Galoosh said, taking the rein of the interrogation away from The Commissioner. "You're a writer. Paint a word picture for us."

"Well," Scott said. "Imagine someone took a 10-ton steel wrecking ball and smashed it into the side of a 100-year-old brick building. Because that's exactly what happened."

"This is not helpful," The Commissioner grumbled and turned to return to his window pose.

"Scott," Galoosh said, "what we need to know is whether or not you think there is a reasonable chance for a baseball game to be played at Fenway Park in the next, oh, I don't know, five to ten days."

Scott nodded solemnly and considered the question thoroughly. "My completely uneducated, uninformed, untrained, unqualified opinion?"

"Yes," Galoosh said. "It's the only one we've got right now."

Scott paused.

"No."

Scott thought someone had hit a bass drum to punctuate his one-word sentence, or was beginning a rimshot for a funny line. Then he realized it was The Commissioner's forehead thumping against the glass of the window.

"Scott," Galoosh said quietly, somberly, as if there had been a death in the room. Scott, whose gaze had fallen to the scalloped pattern of the hotel carpet, looked at him. Galoosh was pointing toward the bathroom.

"Would you like to take a shower before we go downstairs?"

It was only then that Scott realized he was still in his running clothes from earlier that morning, sweat still staining the parts where it pooled, and stinking like a laundry room after a long road trip.

Scott stood with his back against the rear of the banquet room, drumming the fingers of his right hand against the fabric-covered partition that was folded neatly into the wall while his left hand wagged his flimsy reporter's notebook. He'd showered and used the hair dryer in the hotel room upstairs to blow some of the stink off his clothes. No one would care what he was wearing, but he wanted to try to reduce his odor as much as possible for the sake of the other reporters around him. Neither The Commissioner nor Galoosh was in the suite when he finished, and Scott

had figured they had gone downstairs to begin the press conference. But they weren't here, either. Not yet, anyway.

A stage was set up at the front of the room and it included
nothing more than a wooden lectern with the hotel's logo in
brass on the front. A small microphone at the end of a metallic
stem that was bent like a flexible straw jutted from behind the
wooden shelf.

The stage looked out on two banks of chairs that connected
by way of metal hooks, prongs and receptors facing up and
down, depending on which side of the chair they were stationed.
There were six chairs across followed by a small aisle and then
another six chairs. That pattern flowed toward the back of the
room for eight rows. The first two rows were crammed with television reporters who looked over their notes and timed themselves muttering questions under their breath. It would be a gold
star for whichever reporter's voice asked the question that led to
the definitive soundbite of the press conference.

Beyond the television reporters were only a couple of newspaper journalists looking perpetually bored and scattered
throughout the rows, mostly sitting on the aisle or the end of the
rows. The TV folks could go shoulder to shoulder. Back in
Inkville, the general rule was a two-seat gap between you and the
nearest breathing object. Some even extended their sphere by
putting computer bags or backpacks or overcoats on the chairs
next to them. Most of the newspaper sports reporters that Scott
knew, though, stood on the flanks of the room and didn't bother
with the chairs.

Behind the chairs was a larger stage than the one in front.
This one was a platform for the cameras that had arrived to cover
the event. Angry photographers jostled for position, clinging to a
pirate's plank above shark-infested waters, each knowing that a

slip off the safety of the stage would mean their end. Some of the tripods even teetered on demise by having one leg on the stage and two on the carpeted ground, but the camera operators themselves insisted on squeezing aboard their life raft. No toes dangling in the water.

One of the cameramen asked for a mic check and Howard Bowman, a local television sports reporter from Channel 6 known to all as Hobo, jumped from his seat and stood behind the microphone.

"Check, check," Hobo said. "Check, check, check."

Thumbs up from the camera porch. Hobo was just about to return to his seat when another camera operator, this one a woman, asked for a white balance. Hobo held up his legal pad just above the hotel logo but quickly realized that the yellow pages of it would not help anyone. He scanned the room quickly for something that could help the videographers tune their equipment.

"Your shirt," one of the camera creatures said and Hobo stood behind the lectern, flipped his tie over his shoulder, puffed out his chest and pulled the lapels of his blazer to the side. Clark Kent a moment before Superman's arrival.

"Got it!" the camera creatures yelled, but it seemed as if Hobo held the pose for an extra beat longer than was necessary.

Behind the floating cloud of cameras Scott was alone in his notebook-wagging, finger-drumming thoughts when he saw The Professor walk in. There still were a few seats left in the middle, but Scott knew The Professor wouldn't bite. He did take his bag off his shoulder and plopped it on a chair in the back, in the middle of the row where he knew no one would be sitting, and looked back and gave a nod to Scott. Then he found an open spot along the side of the setup and claimed his turf.

"What do you think?"

The voice startled Scott, who was watching The Professor gab with some baseball writers from around the country who were in town for the World Series and wound up covering the Crime of the Century. Scott didn't realize anyone had sauntered up next to him. When he did, he didn't realize who it was. Until he turned slowly so as not to show his jumpiness.

"Hello, Figgy," Scott said out of habit and hated himself for it so much that he corrected himself. "Fig."

"What do you think?"

"What do I think?" Scott asked back and then spilled a series of thoughts as if he'd been waiting all day -- or year -- for someone to ask him that very question. "Well, I think they're not going to play a baseball game tonight. I think they're not going to play another game at Fenway this year, so in other words, never again. I don't know when or how or where they're going to finish the Series. I think the guy they think is a terrorist isn't. I think it's my fault everyone thinks he is. Partially my fault, anyway. Mostly my fault. I think The Commissioner has no idea what he's going to do. I think the police have no idea what they're doing. I think JKL's fingers are going to fall off from dialing my number so often and I think he's going to fire me if I send one more of his calls directly to voicemail. I think The Cure is the most under-appreciated band of the '90s. I think my best source on the team I cover was buried in a beer cup a few days ago and I'm here trying to cover the biggest story in baseball history without much to go on. I think The Professor loves the days such as these when he isn't fully retired more than he loves the ones when he is. I think I look forward to that stage of my life, when I can just ease into a story on a parachute and then be airlifted out. I think I'll never survive in the business long enough to get there. I think Hobo is about 10 years older than me and in far better shape than me. I think he could probably bench about 230 pounds. I think he could kick my ass. I think that holidays should be celebrated on their actual day and not observed on the nearest convenient Monday. I think my idea of fantasy baseball is 162 home games with 1 o'clock starts and no rain delays. I think I hate that I've become a part of the story of what happened this morning. I think I'm tired of saying 'no comment' when other reporters, my friends and colleagues, ask simple questions about what went down and what I saw. I think that I need a publicist to reject the requests I've gotten to appear on *Good Morning, America!*, the *Today* show, *SportsCenter*, and every other wake-me-up gab-fest that thinks they'll get an exclusive by having me on. I think I have voicemails from Oprah on my cellphone and my home phone. Voicemails, Fig. Plural. From Oprah. I think by standing back here, people will get the signal to leave me alone for a while. And, Fig O'Leary, I think you didn't receive that fucking message as clearly as any of the other pathetic drips who are in this room right now and not cowering with their families at home against a fear that they themselves are creating."

Fig digested it all with a slow nod.

"No," he finally said. "I mean Felisha. What do you think about Felisha? Are you going to go to Hawaii and get back to-gether with her?"

Scott swayed up from the wall and turned to face Fig with a disgusted look. He was just about to answer Fig when Sy Ga-loosh stepped onto the stage at the front of the room and tapped the microphone twice so it jiggled at the end of its straw. The thuds and a slight hiss echoed throughout the room.

"Uh, OK," Galoosh said to get everyone's attention, "The Commissioner of Major League Baseball."

The Commissioner stepped to the stage and adjusted the microphone, fiddling with it more out of nervousness than audio concern and returning it to its previous position. Scott grabbed Fig by the arm and led him out the back door of the room just as The Commissioner was thanking everyone for showing up.

As they arrived in the hallway, Scott's mind raced back to the night in college when he had been introduced to Felisha.

Fig took a sip from his red plastic cup and pointed across the room.

"That's her," he said and immediately pulled his arm back for another swig, this one more determined.

"What's her name again? Scott asked.

"Felisha."

"And she's the one from the park last year?"

"Yes."

"Where's her boyfriend?" Scott said while looking around the party at the Phi Kappa Alpha frat house, scanning the flannel-covered grungy wannabes and the sweater-vested pretty boys. "The ear-nibbler? The guy with the dent in his car?"

"They broke up."

Scott turned to Fig.

"You?"

Fig shook his head.

"Her," Fig said.

He pointed in another direction and Scott saw the guy from the park in the corner cozying up to a busty blond in a torn-up sweatshirt and acid-washed jean shorts.

"So let me get this straight," Scott said, going over the plan one more time. "You like this girl so …"

"Love," Fig said. "I love her."

"OK, you love her. But you've never spoken to her."

"Right."

"For over a year you've been in love with her but haven't spoken to her."

"Yup."

"And you want me to ask her out."

"Right."

"And date her for a few weeks."

"Two months max."

"During this time, naturally she'll get to know some of my friends. She'll get to know you."

Fig swigged and nodded.

"Then, after a few weeks, two months max, we break up. I dump her."

"Gently. Amicably."

"And it's your belief that after a brief but appropriate amount of time ..."

"Six to eight days."

"... after six to eight days you will be in position to, um, grab the rebound, I think that's how you put it?"

"Exactly."

"And you are convinced that this is how you will fall in love with each other and get married and have lots of sex and babies and live happily ever after?"

Fig tilted his head back and drained the last drops of his cup. He crushed it in his hand and dropped it carelessly onto the floor and allowed himself a belch.

"I am," he said through the gas escaping his mouth.

"Why don't you just ask her out yourself?"

"She'd say no," Fig said. "She has to get to know me first."

"What if she says no to me?"

"She won't," Fig said with equal and linked confidence in Scott and his plan, helping himself to another plastic cup as a tray of them was circulated around the room by a girl in a bikini with a tattoo of a bottle of Jaggermeister on the upper portion of her left breast.

"What if," Scott said, "she dumps me before I can dump her?"

"She won't," Fig said.

"What if *we* wind up falling in love and get married and have the babies and all that crap?"

"You won't."

"What if?" Scott said. "I'm very charming. Women have a hard time accepting my breakups."

"She's not your type," Fig said.

Scott looked across the room and sipped his own drink. He gave Felisha an up-and-down.

"She might be," Scott said. "The more I look at her ..."

"She's not," Fig said. "Her name is Felisha."

"So?"

"With an S-H. F-e-l-i-s-h-a."

"Not a C? Felicia? Like normal people?"

"No. S. H."

"Ouch."

"Yes," Fig said.

Scott finished his plastic cup.

"Difficult names," Scott said, "are usually difficult people."

Fig nodded.

"It doesn't bother you? The S-H?"

"I like it," Fig said. "It's different. Quirky. Unique."

Scott rolled his eyes.

"It's different, all right."

"So are you going to do it?"

Scott took the half-full plastic cup from Fig's hand and slammed the rest of it down his gullet, crushed the cup and dropped it into what was quickly becoming a pile at their feet.

"I guess if I don't have to spell it and only have to *say* her name, I can do it. But two months?"

"Max."

Scott took a deep breath.

"OK," he said and puffed a burst of air through his wide open mouth into Fig's face for smell approval. "Wish me luck."

"We don't need luck," Fig said. "We have a plan."

Scott had reminded himself of that party 20 or so years earlier a few times in recent days, ever since Fig came back into his life. He knew how manipulative Fig could be. Charmingly manipulative. Not pushy. Not threatening. But the kind of guy who made you *want* to do things for him even though you didn't want to do them. And now that both Fig and Felisha were in orbit around him, Scott knew he had to be strong to withstand their combined gravitational pull.

It was easier with Fig, given his betrayal and the falling out that crushed their relationship like those plastic cups that landed on the floor between them that night. Relationships -- particularly between men who have dozens of acquaintances and pals and buddies but few true friends – are plastic cups. You can crumple them and toss them on the floor. They can sit in landfills for centuries, never breaking down, never disintegrating. Just buried under garbage and time and wounds and whatever other crap was dumped on top of them.

Scott hated Fig. Their friendship may have been long gone, rotted to nothingness. Their relationship, though, that was not so biodegradable. Scott knew that, so he proceeded carefully with Fig in the hallway just outside the press conference.

"What's with the get-up?" Fig asked Scott as he was being

pulled toward something close to privacy. "Halloween was yesterday."

"I was running," Scott said. "This morning, I was running."

"Running?" Fig said with disbelief. "You? Well, I mean,
good for you. What do you do, like 11-minute miles?"

"Nine," Scott said.

"Nice!"

"What do you want?"

"Oh," Fig said, refocused on their conversation from just a moment ago. "I want to know what you're thinking about Felisha."

"You set that up! You tried to set us up again, you shit!"

"She asked me where you'd be and I told her."

"Right. Innocent Fig O'Leary."

"She wants to get back together with you and save your marriage. I felt I needed to help."

"Yeah, you were real good at helping her after I left."

"Well, you know I've always just wanted Felisha to be happy."

"And you think she was happy that night with you?"

"No," Fig said. "No, she wasn't. And that's why I went there."

Scott collected himself so his shouting could not be heard in
the adjacent press conference.

"Fig," he said as calmly as he could, "You're -- she's --
you're both trying to save a marriage that no longer exists."

"It'll always exist," Fig said calmly, peacefully. He never
raised his voice when he argued. It infuriated Scott. "Everything
that's ever been exists. It may not be alive now, but don't say it
doesn't exist."

"OK, Kierkegaard," Scott said. "Listen to what I am telling
you. I hate her. I hate you. I hate you and her. You wanted to
know what I think? That's what I think. It's what I know."

"Do you believe in signs, Scott?"

"Like what, divine intervention?"

"If that's how you want to see it."

"You want me to consider the possibility that all of these crazy things happening in my life right now, all of it, is the universe's way of getting me back together with Felisha?"

"Can't you see that your paths have been brought together?" Fig reasoned. "That you and Felisha were meant to meet at this intersection of your life?"

Scott gathered himself as best he could and took it step by step.

"So God had the Red Sox make the playoffs,"

"Maybe. God or something else. Whatever you believe."

"And God brought the Sox to the World Series."

"Possibly."

"And God made it snow in Chicago, made Buster Sinclair take a line drive off his skull, and convinced that fucking Polish moron to swing his wrecking ball through the stadium ... just so I could get back together with Felisha?"

"Nuts, isn't it?"

Scott's eyes widened and he nodded vigorously in agreement. He collected himself before proceeding.

"Why does she even want me back? She was as miserable as I was in our marriage."

"You know how she hates to lose," Fig said.

Right, Scott thought. *Even if it's with a guy she wouldn't vote for.*

"You're batshit crazy," Scott said. "The two of you are. And you both think you can control me. But you can't." He began to walk away.

"Wait," Fig said, and this time he grabbed Scott's arm and pulled him. "Let me see your phone."

"I'm not giving you my phone."

"Give me your phone."

"Why?"

"Because," Fig said, "I want to see if Felisha's number is still in your address book. If you were truly over her, you'd have erased it by now. Anyone who was not in love with someone would have done that."

"No."

Fig was in Scott's head.

"Give me your phone," Fig said.

"No."

"If she's gone," Fig said, "you have nothing to worry about."

"She's gone," Scott said.

"Good. Gimme."

Scott handed it over, unsure who was calling whose bluff at that moment.

"So if she's not in here, I'll leave you alone. You can go about your life. But if she is in here …"

Fig looked at Scott to see if he would squirm. Scott looked at Fig, trying to appear as if he were holding a royal flush.

"… if she is in here," Fig continued, "we're calling her right now and you and her are going to meet and discuss your future."

"Fine," Scott conceded.

"OK then."

Fig typed F-E-L-I-S-H-A into the window at the top of the address book and hit search.

No results, the phone told him.

Fig nodded in defeat. He started to hand the phone back to Scott, who reached out to accept it, but just before the transaction, Fig pulled it back. He opened the address book again and typed in the name with one small difference.

F-E-L-I-C-I-A.

It popped up. Home, cell, email, the whole little digital rolodex card filled out. Scott hung his head.

"Fuck."

"I should have known you'd spell it the way you wanted it to be spelled," Fig said.

"So what?" Scott said. "She's my son's mother! There's nothing wrong with me having that number in my phone."

But Scott knew. And he knew Fig knew. There were plenty of nights in the last several years when he laid awake in bed staring at his phone, ready to swipe Felisha -- or Felicia -- or both -- out of his life. A few times he even mustered the courage to do it, but each time the damn phone asked him if he was sure. The phone. It asked him if he was sure. He never was. So he'd cancel the command and Felisha would go on living in his hand-held black book.

"I'm calling her," Fig said.

"Go ahead," Scott shrugged nonchalantly. "Knock yourself out."

"No," Fig said, "I'm calling and you're talking."

Scott stood with his lips clutched tightly. His head nodded a bit on his neck, not a nod of approval but the nod of a man weighing his options and considering his retreats. It was more of a bounce than a nod, as if Curly Neal were drumming his scalp against a basketball court floor.

"I'm calling now," Fig said, giving Scott the possibility to stop him.

Scott did not.

Fig hit the button, listened for the first ring, and then handed the phone back to Scott. Scott put the phone to his ear but Fig objected.

"Oh, no," he said. "Speakerphone. Until she picks up. So I know you aren't hanging up."

Scott touched that button.

The phone rang a second time. Then a third. And a fourth. And finally, the electronically-produced voice.

"You have reached the mailbox of ... Felisha Findle (in her own voice) ... To leave a numeric message, enter it now. To leave a voicemail, please wait for the beep."

Beep.

Scott hung up.

"I'm not leaving a message," he told Fig.

"It doesn't matter now," Fig said with a grin. "She'll know you called."

Scott slumped against the hallway wall, manipulated by the Great Fig O'Leary once again, and tried to come to grips with the enormity of what had just happened. Felisha would see the call. She'd know Scott was thinking about her. Maybe she'd already erased his number, he thought, and she wouldn't recognize it? No shot, he thought. He was in it now.

Just then the doors to the press conference swung open. The Commissioner walked out, followed by Sy Galoosh, and they headed quickly to an elevator that was waiting to take them upstairs. The reporters began filing out of the room too. The Professor walked out with the rest of the scribes, most of them talking nervously into their phones or thumbing away at their mini keypads. He approached Fig and Scott in the hallway.

"What happened?" Scott asked. "What did he say?"

"Are they going to play the game?" Fig asked.

"Boys," The Professor said with a smile, "we're going back to Chicago."

CHAPTER ELEVEN

They asked if he wanted to play with them, but he just smiled that vague grin of incomprehension, waved politely, and kept walking.

"Probably doesn't speak English," Fig said.

"Well, it is a public course," The Judge said, unsure why he needed to defend the linguistics of another golfer, especially when they had not been impugned with any severity. Fig was right. He probably didn't speak English. He didn't look as if he did, anyway. Or he couldn't hear through the wind and the hood of his blue nylon poncho, the drawstring secured under his chin in a floppy bow tie, the oval frame not quite fitting his round brown face. Regardless, it worked out fine with him playing ahead of them.

A fierce wind and a cold misty rain sogged the grass and turned the bottom six inches of their trouser legs dark and heavy, like paper plates after two helpings of baked beans. But even on a miserable March day, they weren't alone. Others addicted to the sport slogged along the fairways, constantly scraping excess mud from the rubber spikes on their shoes, looking up at the gray clouds galloping the gray sky, searching for a par or a birdie in the early-season gloom.

Because of the saturated ground, which had just recently shed its final coating of grimy, late-winter snow, carts were not allowed on the course. The walking groups with bags slung over their shoulders, or sometimes pulled on handcarts, bottlenecked for the first several holes, mostly because of the par-3s that dominated the early landscape. By the sixth hole, the long par-5, they began spacing out so the waiting at the tee boxes was not interminable. Most groups played nine holes and then retreated to their cars, given that the ninth green and tenth tee were positioned next to the parking lot.

There were not enough golfers to enforce the traditional foursomes. Fig and The Judge played by themselves. Behind them was a threesome of older men, one of whom carried a small collapsible aluminum chair in his bag so he could sit and catch his breath after every 100 yards or so of walking. The Judge had seen the contraption, named the Spring-Loaded Squatter, in the magazines and catalogs that indulged gadget-loving golfers with alliterative apparatus and unnecessary technology. He'd even thought of buying a Squatter but instead decided to purchase the Laser Level, a device that reads the slope of a green and estimates the path of a successful putt. Like most items in those catalogs, it didn't work nearly as well as it should have, and as The Judge saw the simple efficiency of the Squatter in action, he regretted his choice.

That single brown-skinned golfer, rain poncho tied tight under his jaw, played quickly, sometimes dawdling with a second ball but never as an inconvenience to Fig and The Judge. He was short and heavyset, but not obese enough to stand out among the retired and the leisure-minded who frequented golf courses. He was dressed too neatly to be an employee at the course; those guys wear nondescript military olive-green clothes day after day so they retain the stains of work, but his coverings were bright, crisp, and imprinted with well-known logos.

The Judge had noticed the inconsistency of his tools immediately, which made him think he was new to the game and had bought the clubs at garage sales or swap meets. Most beginners hesitate to spend the money for a full set of matching irons, and The Judge could tell from the different types and colors of grips -- reddish-brown leather, black synthetics, one wrapped in electrical tape -- that these were either hand-me-downs or secondhand. But the bag was new, bold red with white pockets, and a conspicuous driver with an oversized head roughly the size and shape of a hefty Kaiser roll was obviously new and contradicted the others. Like most novices, he clearly was long ball-obsessed, eschewing his short game for towering, glamorous tee shots. He kept the big club covered in a leather sheath, but The Judge recognized it from the catalogs as the Halloway 7500 Big Bomber with a fused titanium shaft, just on the market at the end of last season. It retailed for almost $400. He had no opportunity to use it on the early holes because of the par-3s, but he seemed to hit a solid drive on the long sixth hole.

The Judge was playing terribly, slicing drives and topping long irons through the mushy turf. Fig, who bragged about the hours and money he had spent at the indoor driving range three towns over during the winter, was sizzling. His drives were straight and true. His approaches were on target. And even his putting, always a flawed aspect of his game, was strong. After 12 holes, he was four strokes under par without a bogey. The Judge was plus-14.

They moved along quite quickly and arrived at the secluded 13th tee, the point farthest from the clubhouse, only to see the lone brown-skinned, blue-slickered duffer playing the hole.

"There's not even a bench to sit on and wait," The Judge moaned, the dampness beginning to creep into his knees and lower back, thinking again about the Squatter.

"So hit," Fig said, impatient to keep going. He had honors after sinking a 17-foot birdie putt on 12, but he was willing to forfeit that right to keep the game moving.

"He's too close," The Judge answered. "Wait 'til he gets on
the green at least."

"Just hit," Fig coaxed. "He's at least 200 yards away. Besides, the way you're hitting, the safest place for him is right
down the middle."

The Judge hesitated a moment and surveyed the deteriorating
sky, hunting for a glint of sun before deciding it would be smart-
er to play than stand in the rain. He reached into his pocket and
pulled out a tee and the Bullet brand golf ball he favored. He
fussed with the few buds of grass in the launching area and
plugged the tee into ground so saturated that water oozed to the
surface. It reminded him of the Botox injections he'd seen on a
news program the previous night. He stood over the balancing
ball, took a practice swing, inched closer to the target and swung
in earnest. It felt great. His first solid hit of the season.

"Uh-oh," Fig muttered under his breath, quickly realizing the
golf ball was heading directly for the duffer, who was now 250
yards ahead of them, pacing the right side of the fairway.

"Fore!" The Judge yelled. "Fore!"

"*Cuatro!*" Fig hollered with bilingual ferocity. The man
ahead of them continued walking, but he turned just in time to
have the ball greet the side of his skull with a thud they could
hear even from their impressive distance. He pirouetted ab-
ruptly before his knees buckled like a drunken figure skater's,
the golf bag drooping from his right shoulder and spilling its
assortment of clubs and extra balls. Finally, after what seemed
like minutes but must have been only a second or two, the
man collapsed.

"Let's go!" The Judge yelled, not sure if he wanted to run away toward the parking lot or toward the downed golfer to offer assistance. He was a few paces down the fairway when Fig shouted: "Hang on a second!"

The Judge turned around and ducked just as Fig completed his swing, driving his tee shot 20 yards farther than his and closer to the center of the fairway.

"Okay," Fig said, sliding his driver back into his bag, "let's go." They arrived at the golfer, who was lying face-up, several flecks of recently clipped green grass blades attached to his wet cheeks. A trickle of blood ran from the corner of his mouth, zigzagging through his stubblish beard and the beading rain, collecting against the still-tight poncho hood that routed it down his neck. His eyes were closed.

"He's dead," The Judge said. "He's fucking dead. What are we going to do?"

The Judge couldn't get a signal on his cellphone to call 911. Fig pointed out that it would take at least five minutes to run back to the clubhouse to use the phone in the pro shop. Then, by the time authorities arrived, there would be statements to issue and forms to fill out. Too many questions to answer.

"I have to be in court in two hours," The Judge sighed. "I can't stick around for this. He's dead. Let's just leave him here."

The golfer groaned and shivered a fierce, wretched convulsion. Fig reached down to touch his neck, feel for a pulse.

"It's very faint," he said. "I don't think he's gonna make it."

"Let's just leave," The Judge said. "Or play on. Let the geezers behind us find him."

Fig's gloved hand reached into the man's pocket and fished out a wallet. He looked at the driver's license. Manuel Torpodo. The name Manny was stitched onto his poncho as well as his golf bag.

"Maybe they'll think he just had a heart attack or something," The Judge said.

"No, they'll know it was a blow to the head," Fig said, standing straight now, only his head bent over the dying man. "They'll know it was us."

Then Fig turned to The Judge with a sneer of self-preservation: "They'll know it was you."

"Me? Me?!"

"You know you're not supposed to hit up on a golfer within your range. It says so on the sign at the pro shop. Common golf course etiquette."

"You made me. 'Go ahead and hit,' you said."

Visions of lawsuits or even a manslaughter trial suddenly filled The Judge's head along with a thousand other rambles of thought. If he makes it, he'll be able to identify us. If he's dead, they'll realize it was from a golf ball to the head. The police will know whoever was playing between the old men and Manny is the culprit. Did he have a motive? An alibi? Would he lawyer up? Could a judge lawyer up? Was that an inherent conflict of interest?

"No one made you do anything," Fig said slowly and faintly. He picked up the ball that had struck Manny and tossed it to The Judge, underhanded. The Judge pocketed the Bullet without thinking, suddenly noticing Fig's calm. It wasn't as if he went through these traumas once a week. Rather, he was in what athletes call "the zone." The Judge was zoneless.

"What am I going to do?" The Judge asked, almost pleading.

Well," Fig said with a contemplative softness, scratching his chin with his gloved hand in a thinking manner, as if deciding whether to lay up or try to hit over a fairway bunker, "I suppose if it were to look like an accident, or more of an accident than it actually was, we wouldn't need to do anything."

The Judge's blinking eyes tried to keep up. Manny's moan mingled with the wind to create an odd, surprisingly mellow tone.

"If he was dead when we got to this hole, and we played down the opposite side of the fairway, no one would suspect you in anything, nor would they expect you to see him and do anything about it."

"But," The Judge said, slowly catching on to the plan Fig was laying out in front of him, "we'd have to be sure he was dead."

Fig nodded.

Apple trees separated the fairways that ran parallel to each other, and they were just a few feet from a pathetic-looking one. The Judge scooped his arms under Manny's shoulders and dragged him under the tree, then flipped him over so his face squished in the mud and bubbles emerged from his nostril with every labored, periodic breath. Then he reached into the apple tree, macerated by the winter, and tugged off a large, dead limb. Manny groaned one more gurgle of consciousness before The Judge walloped him with the branch on the side of his head. Six times. But the decaying limb crumbled and did not deliver the slaying force necessary. The Judge needed something stronger. Something solid. Something made of ... titanium.

He picked up Manny's driver, which still had its leather cover over the head, and it felt good in his hands as he wiggled it to sense the bend of the shaft. It definitely was worth the retail price of four bills; a club like that could take three or four strokes off a guy's game. He squeezed the leather grip and muddy juice wrung out through his fingers. He looked back toward the tee box, checked in several other directions, then delivered the blow that killed Manny. He heard his skull collapse, but just like hitting a solid shot, he didn't feel the impact. It was strangely satisfying. Manny must have sensed it coming because he gave a short, gasping, hiccupping "*No!*" just before the oversized driver met his hooded head.

"I guess he does speak English," Fig said with a how-'bout-that nod and lip purse, sliding the wallet back into Manny's pocket.

Manny's cleated feet gave one final twitch before the moaning and the breathing stopped. No one would mistake this for a heart attack. Any coroner worth his bone saw would know it was a blow to the head that killed Manny, and not one delivered by a simple golf ball.

"'No' is the same in English and Spanish," The Judge told Fig. "That doesn't prove anything."

He put the driver in his golf bag and grabbed another branch from the sad apple tree, flipping it on Manny's body as to look random, with as much remorse as a drop shot after hitting a ball in a water hazard.

"The wind must have blown this old limb down and it hit him in the head. We played down the left side of the fairway so we never saw him lying here like this. Dead."

"Dead," Fig said.

"That's right," The Judge replied, cool as the March winds. "A terrible accident. This old tree should have been taken down years ago."

"Negligence," Fig agreed.

The Judge began walking toward the green when an "Ahem" from Fig stopped him.

"You're not going to leave that divot, are you?"

Manny's dragged heels carved two parallel grooves through the grass. Had it been a dry day, the short rough would have been permanently scarred. Luckily the rain left the turf malleable and he was able to sculpt it flat with a few swipes of his shoe.

By the time The Judge completed one final survey of the area to make sure everything was in place, Fig was addressing his ball in the middle of the fairway. His pitching wedge knocked the ball onto the green, but he two-putted for par. The Judge offered him the use of his Laser Level, but he shooed it away with a frustrated hand. They shortly arrived at the 14th tee, a par-5 dogleg. They checked behind them to make sure the threesome hadn't arrived at the body. They hadn't. The Judge gave himself a par on the 13th, just to have a completed scorecard if they ever had to prove their story. Fig at first argued he should take a bogey, but relented.

The Judge surprised himself with the poise and newfound confidence with which he reached into his pocket and pulled out the Bullet, wiped it against his pant leg, and placed it on the tee.

"This hole always gives me trouble," he said to Fig, staring down the long swath of green before him. "Maybe I'll try my new driver."

He pulled the cover off the club, only to find the initials M.T. etched on the head.

"Those letters still stare at him every time he addresses a ball with the club," Fig told Scott the night he relayed the story, several years later, when the two still were close enough to share such intimacies. Scott thought then, as he did now, recalling that evening, that the tale should be dismissed as fabrication but an interesting fictionalization of just how manipulative and devious Fig could be.

"They don't remind him of that terrible day when the rain was whipping and the clouds roared past like stock cars," Fig had said. "And they don't remind him of Manny -- the golfer whose death was, after an inquiry, blamed on the rotting apple tree and a bellow of wind -- though they are his initials and this was his driver."

"No," Fig continued, "he looks at M.T. before each drive and recalls the swing that led him to the club, the free, easy, unthinking, unsuspecting, nothing-to-lose swing that launched a perfect shot. Hands back, head down, knees bent. Manny just happened to be in an imperfect position."

Fig took a quick swig of his drink.

"Anyway," Fig concluded, "it's the only club that never slices on him."

"You're full of crap," Scott told him.

"Maybe."

"You're no killer."

"I didn't kill anyone."

"Who is this Judge?"

"I can't tell you," Fig grinned.

"Why not?"

"Because I promised him I would never tell anyone."

"You just told me."

"I didn't tell you his name."

"It's another bullshit story, anyway. A judge? Golf? You made that up."

"Think that," Fig shrugged.

"This Judge killed a guy and you have to keep his name a secret?"

"Yup."

"And you don't write it?"

"Nope."

"Why?"

"Because now he owes me one."

Fig spoke the last sentence with such calm, such a lack of emotion, that it gave Scott a chill then. And now. Even if he still did not believe it.

CHAPTER TWELVE

Just as Scott, Fig and The Professor were drawing straws in the lobby of the Sheraton to see whose car they would take to Chicago – a formality, given that Fig's license had been revoked and The Professor did not own a car, but one that at least made the two impossibilities feel they were part of a fair process -- they felt the whoosh of cameras heading back into the ballroom where The Commissioner's press conference had just been held.

"What the hell is going on now?" The Professor asked.

"The mayor's gonna talk," one of the burly camera operators said as he swung his tripod dangerously close to clipping Scott's knees.

"About the game?" The Professor followed up.

"Who knows."

Scott and The Professor followed the throng into the room. Fig walked in a different direction. Per usual.

The cameras still were getting into position when the mayor walked in with a half dozen other moderately-suited officials who appeared to be in charge of various things at various times. The mayor stepped right to the bank of microphones, stretching up on his toes so his round little face could be seen over the top of them.

"OK," he said casually, "we wanted to do this here because we knew all of you would still be in position after the World Series announcement. Which we are deeply upset about, by the way. So let me just say now, on the record, that Game Seven should be played in Boston. The Red Sox earned the right to host the game, and that achievement should be honored."

The mayor either didn't realize or disregarded the fact that homefield advantage in the World Series now was determined not by any achievement but by online fan voting that took place in August.

"Anyway," he continued, "the reason we're here. This guy, uh, Cheez-wiz or whatever."

"Szczesny," a sour-looking aide said patiently.

"Right. Szczesny. He didn't do nothing. I mean, yeah, he did knock a hole in Fenway. But he didn't do it on purpose. Actually, he did. But not with malice. What I'm trying to say is it was a miscommunication. An accident. We're convinced he's not a terrorist, as some in the media have libeled him."

"Labeled," the aide corrected.

"Right. Labeled."

Those two word stiffened Scott's spine: terrorist and libel. It was bad enough that he'd been unfairly linked to labeling Szczesny a terrorist. This now made it worse. The label was wrong.

"Again," the mayor said, as if kicking Scott in the other shin, "not a terrorist."

The room buzzed. The mayor tried to hush the reporters with two hands and looked as if he were banging the keys of an invisible piano while doing so.

"So," the mayor continued as casually as is he had gone off the menu and ordered the shrimp fra diavolo at his favorite Southie restaurant, "Boston is back open. The airports, the train stations, the roads. There is no imminent danger to the citizens of this city. And no charges will be pressed against Mr., um, uh, you know, Mr. Wrecking Ball Guy."

Two dozen questions were shouted at once.

"Special Agent Daly will answer any further questions you may have," the mayor said, giving him a perfunctory pat on the shoulder before skipping off the podium with Cary Grant style and heading out the door.

Daly had been through the process plenty of times.

"My name is Special Agent Steven Daly, that's Steven with a 'V' and Daly with no I and no E," he said. "I'll be happy to answer your questions as accurately and honestly as I can, but I'd also like to do so in an orderly fashion."

Remarkably, Daly was able to wrangle the media herd into some semblance of a direction. Scott tapped The Professor on the arm and head-juked at the door to signal that it was time to go. As they were leaving the room, Scott looked down the hallway and saw Fig speaking with The Commissioner and Sy Galoosh near a window at the far end of the corridor. He couldn't afford to spend much time figuring out what they might be talking about, though, because his mind was tugged back by the first question for Special Agent Daly.

It was about the presidential candidates. About their whereabouts.

"In all the chaos of the day," Daly said, "we seem to have, um, lost track of them. We presume they are safe. Just ... misplaced at the present moment."

No one in that room could have imagined that Brandt and Ott -- only one of them dressed in his own clothes -- and their most trusted advisers still were in the storage room two floors directly below the podium. Certainly not Scott, whose thoughts now wandered to his ex-wife. He pulled out his phone to try to text her, to see where she was. But he stopped. If he didn't know better, Scott would have thought Fig himself had put those thoughts inside his head.

The Sheraton had plenty of outlets and free Wi-Fi and a chair with a table. In other words, it was a reporter's heaven. That the table and chair and outlet and Internet signal happened to be in the hotel's bar, well, that just made things all the better. Scott set up a base camp and got to work, trying to write a coherent story about the happenings of the day. He had to remind himself that the events from that morning, while they seemed distant history, had never actually been in a printed newspaper.

News reporters had pounced on the Szczesny storyline and all aspects of the lockdown and subsequent unlocking. Fig had been tapped to re-write the obituary for Fenway, adding the final cause of death as only he could. He also was trying to get the first interview with Szczesny, but no one believed he'd be able to pull that off. That left baseball on Scott's plate -- which suited him perfectly fine -- and he was just sending in the final version of the World Series' exodus to Chicago when he sensed looming behind him. He turned.

"Hell of a day," Sy Galoosh said. "May we?"

"Sure," Scott said, kicking out the empty seats next to him. "I'm running a tab."

"So are we," The Commissioner said, grabbing the attention of the bartender with a quick hand wave. Scott pushed the empty plate that until recently held his Cobb salad dinner toward the inner half of the bar proper, both to make room for his new guests and to signal that he was finished with it.

The bartender swapped the plate for two drinks.

"It'll all be over with tomorrow," The Commissioner said,

raising his glass. "To tomorrow."

"That's what we thought yesterday," Scott pointed out, spoiling the toast as The Commissioner put his glass to his lips. The Commissioner paused to consider Scott's statement, then swallowed the entire contents of the tumbler.

"I've been out of the loop a bit," Scott said. "Any word on the candidates? The election is tomorrow."

A booming voice interrupted them from across the bar before there was an answer.

"I hope you're enjoying your beverage, Mr. Commissioner!"

It was Roger Fleiss, from the network.

"It may be your last," Fleiss added, slowly marching across the room to join the trio. "As The Commissioner, that is."

"Roger," The Commissioner said. "We've been expecting you."

"I'll bet!" Fleiss thundered. "It wasn't bad enough that you tried to put your game up against my presidential debates. No, that wasn't enough for a dipshit like you. You had to go and schedule the most dramatic Game Seven in baseball history for the same night as the closest presidential election in a generation."

"It's being taken care of, Roger," Galoosh said.

"It's being taken care of? That's what you tell me? I have to move 200 people and a $20 million production unit from Boston to Chicago in less than 24 hours, and you tell me it's being taken care of? Well, shit, I had no idea. I should be down here with you guys drinking and celebrating, then."

"There were circumstances," The Commissioner said.

"Yeah, the terrorist," Fleiss said. "The terrorist who wasn't."

He looked at Scott and frowned.

"Roger," Galoosh said, "it's being taken care of. Just get your people to Chicago."

"Why? So we can spend the entire broadcast updating the

country on election results and I can spend the night having news directors screaming at me over the phone about breaking in between pitches because the fucking polls in fucking Alabama have fucking closed?"

The Commissioner turned in his chair and faced Fleiss.

"All I can tell you now, Roger, is that it's under control," he said. "It's being taken care of."

"I don't know what that means."

"You will," Galoosh said calmly. "By the time you leave Boston, you will."

Scott didn't know what it meant, either. But he didn't think long about deciphering the clues. His attention was being yanked by the clamoring in the lobby just over Fleiss' jagged shoulder and past his twitching left eye. There was some yelling and then the burst of LED light that comes only from a flock of television cameras being turned on and pointed in one direction at the same time.

Fleiss sensed the commotion as well and turned to investigate for himself.

Wandering across the lobby, as confused by their whereabouts and the sensation they were stirring as if they had just emerged from a time machine, were Emerson Ott, Henry Brandt, and several of their staff members. Scott likely was the only one who could name the woman walking next to Brandt.

They were coming straight at him. To the bar. Reporters doused them with questions. Actually, it was one question in many variations. Where were you? Where have you been? What happened? When did you get here? How did you get here? Oddly, no one asked the most obvious and pressing question: What the hell was Brandt wearing?

They crossed the threshold of the bar, and for some reason, the cameras and reporters stopped, as if they could not cross the border from public space to private. Brandt and Ott were staring at the televisions on the wall over the bar, but they seemed unsatisfied with what they were seeing. Finally, Brandt looked at Scott. Perhaps there was some flicker of recognition. More likely, he just happened to be where Brandt's eyes landed.

"What's the score?"

"The score?" Scott asked back.

"Of the game," Ott said impatiently. "The World Series. Game Seven. What's the score?"

Fleiss, Galoosh and The Commissioner just stared back at the candidates, one of whom would be elected president the following day. Scott, though, turned his gaze toward Felisha. He watched her as she tapped away at her phone with little CPR finger taps, bringing the gadget back to life after it had been flatlining the whole day.

"There was no signal," she said, frustrated, to no one in particular.

"There's Wi-Fi here," Scott offered instinctively.

"Thanks."

It was a conversation between strangers.

"There we go," she said, pulling her fluttering hand away from the phone. Scott could see the device vibrate continuously in her hands. How many phone calls and emails must a high-ranking aide to a presidential candidate receive the day before the election, he wondered, imagining the entire flood of them coming in at once. The good thing, Scott realized, was that his call -- Fig's call -- would be lost in the data tsunami. Scott was relieved. Until he saw Felisha's eyes widen at one particular vibration.

And then she blushed ever so slightly.

Scott recognized it at once, the same flush of involuntary pink that would flash in her cheeks when they would be out to dinner as a couple and he would gently place his hand on her thigh under the table or, for a darker hue, when he would send her raunchy, suggestive texts from one side of a boring cocktail party to the other explaining his plans for the rest of the night once they were able to be alone. Scott knew that in the haystack of emails and phone calls and texts and messages, she somehow had stumbled upon his needle of a missed call.

He braced for her to raise her head, but the color quickly left her face and she returned to her vibrations. They both knew, though. She didn't have to make eye contact. She knew and was thrilled. He knew she knew and was sickened.

It felt as if Scott had been lost in non-verbal communication with Felisha for 20 minutes, but just as dreams have a time of their own, it was only seconds. Scott realized the altered pace of his thoughts when he finally heard The Commissioner speak to Brandt and Ott.

"We had to postpone the game," he said.

The two men looked at him quizzically.

"Why?" Brandt asked.

"There was a situation," Galoosh said. "At Fenway. The game will be played tomorrow."

"Tomorrow," Ott repeated.

"In Chicago," Fleiss said.

"Chicago?" Brandt blurted. "What the fuck?"

Felisha, still staring at her hand-held screen, put her other hand on Brandt's shoulder to calm him down. Brandt looked at Scott again. Apparently he was a trustworthy semi-stranger.

"What's going on?"

Scott was about to answer, but he realized he could do better than half-heartedly rehashing it for the ninth time that day.

"Have a seat here, Governor," he said, getting to his feet and offering his barstool to Brandt before directing the candidate to his open laptop and punching a document open on the desktop. "Read this."

The Governor leaned in and began to scan the article Scott had written and just filed. He got through the first paragraph before gasping out loud again.

"Chicago?" he reiterated.

Felisha, who was too consumed by her BlackBerry to notice the change in positioning, instinctively put her hand on the shoulder next to her to calm her candidate but quickly realized Brandt had switched places with Scott.

Scott regarded her touch as he would a spider, easing away from it without making any sudden movements. Felisha pulled her hand back after a quick meeting of Scott's angry-wide eyes and her own.

Brandt still was scouring the story, trying to piece together the jigsawed day. Ott had huddled with his adviser for a quick powwow, and in a matter of minutes he was heading back to the mystical barrier between the bar and the lobby. The lights of the cameras came back on and Ott, his hair combed and tie straightened, lied to the lenses and hovering microphones about how he had been absent most of the day but had been working hard with The Commissioner (a quick glance over his shoulder to the man himself sitting at the bar for emphasis) to bring Game Seven to Chicago.

"If a man wants to be president," he said, nodding in agreement with himself, "he has to remember what's important to the regular folks. Sure they worry about jobs and health care and other policies. But when it comes down to it, what they really want to do at the end of the day is sit back and watch a ballgame. And I'm the candidate who is giving them that. In Chicago."

Brandt got up from the barstool.

"We have to say something," he said to Felisha. "What should we say?"

"Nothing," she said.

"Nothing?"

"We can't," she said.

"The cameras are right there," Brandt said, extending his arm almost halfway to the nearest one. "And we don't have anything to say?"

"Sir," Felisha said, "are you forgetting something?"

She gave him an up and down with her eyes and Brandt suddenly remembered the misfit T-shirt and sweats he was wearing. He turned back to the bar and punched the hardwood surface with such force that Scott's laptop jumped up.

Felisha then turned to Scott.

"We need to talk," she said.

"We have nothing to talk about," he said, feeling it came out a bit too defensively. He wished he could have a mulligan, a do-over. Say the same words, but with a different tone.

"Scott," she said, "we need to talk. But later. After I take care of this."

Felisha guided Brandt out a side entrance to the bar while the cameras focused on Ott, who was regaling them with the tale of their escape from the basement. The truth was that they had been found and released by a bellhop who was putting away a stack of chairs from the afternoon's press conferences, but somehow Ott made it sound as if they had swum from Alcatraz to San Francisco, then crawled through a tunnel that had been dug by Steve McQueen himself.

Before they disappeared, Felisha turned over her shoulder to reiterate her demand to Scott.

"We need to talk," she said. "Tonight."

Then her cheeks flashed that pink that Scott had at one time found so irresistible, that he once strove to generate whenever possible.

"Call me," she said. "You have the number."

Ott was still at the main barrier between bar and lobby when a slender body seemed to slither its way past the enormous crowd. Staring into the lights, it was hard to determine details, but Scott heard the voice as the oblivious person excuse-me'd and pardon-me'd his way through, a motorcycle zig-zagging past bumper-to-bumper traffic.

"Scotty!" Fig yelled.

"Hello, Fig," Scott said. "I was just thinking about you."

He didn't bother to mention he was thinking of punching him in the teeth and stomping his skull for dialing Felisha's number earlier in the day.

"Good," Fig said, pulling up close to Scott so he didn't have to shout. "I got him."

"Got who?"

"Szczesny."

"They let him go," Scott said.

"I know," Fig said. "Turns out he's not really a terrorist."

Scott closed his eyes to regain whatever patience he had left. He decided a change of direction was in order.

"Do you know The Commissioner and Sy Galoosh?" he asked innocently. He'd seen them talking earlier but played dumb.

Fig nodded at them.

"Skip," he said to The Commissioner.

"And this is Roger Fleiss," Scott added.

Fig didn't nod to him.

"So this guy doesn't even speak English," Fig said. "Doesn't know the difference between a base and a ball, never mind that the two of them go together. He just goes to work like he's supposed to, trying to build his American Dream one demolition at a time. It's poetry, really."

"How'd you get him?" Scott asked.

"I know his lawyer," Fig said. "He set us up with a translator. The guy spilled everything. It's an amazing story."

"You just missed Felisha," Scott said, his head mad-teacupping from one drama to the next at such a dizzying pace that he was unable to keep up with the narratives.

"I know," Fig said. "I saw her and Brandt walking out."

"Roger is pissed," Scott said, pointing to the network czar. "Because Game Seven will be played tomorrow, the same time as the election."

"Haven't you heard?" Fig asked, pulling back from Scott to size him up.

Just then every phone in the hotel seemed to buzz, ring, tingle, flutter, sing, dance or transform into whatever jostling effect it was programmed to when a situation arose. A situation in which news was being transmitted instantly through every feed and news agency at the same time. The last time Scott remembered this happening, the eerie feeling that something momentous was going to be on his screen when he looked at it, was when that SEAL team killed Bin Laden. He looked first at the others in the lobby and bar staring wide-mouthed at their devices before picking his up.

He didn't have to unlock his screen. The message came through as an alert, a simple sentence.

SCOTUS delays presidential election due to candidates' prolonged absence.

Scott looked up at Fig.

"They canceled Election Day?"

"Postponed, not canceled," Fig said. "You know the difference. They postponed it. Like a rainout."

Scott looked at The Commissioner and Sy Galoosh, who did not seem at all surprised by the developments. He looked at Fleiss, who was smiling for the first time in a decade and gave a wink to The Commissioner.

"You canceled a presidential election for a baseball game?" Scott asked.

"Postponed, not canceled, Scott," responded The Commissioner. "Besides, do you think I have that kind of power?"

"No," Scott said, staring at Fig. "But I wasn't asking you."

"The Chief Justice of the Supreme Court is the only one who does have that power," The Commissioner said.

"It's postponed. A week," Galoosh said. "Don't worry, Scott. Democracy will survive."

Fig began telling Scott that the idea of holding elections on the first Tuesday of November was antiquated anyway. "It comes from when America was an agrarian country," he said, suddenly a social studies teacher. Scott just stared at him blankly, a social studies student. "November was after the harvest so most farmers were free, and they did it on Tuesdays so no one would have to travel on Sundays to get to the county seat for the vote."

As if his implication were not clear, Fig added: "Religion. It was big back then."

Scott reached for some handle of mental stability. He found none. All he could grab was Fig.

"So," Fig said with a big smile, "did Felisha see that you called?"

"I didn't call her," Scott said. "You did."

"Are you going to see her tonight?"

"This is, without a doubt, the worst day of my life," Scott said.

"Hey, that reminds me," Fig said. "Szczesny's lawyer. I had to do him a favor to get the interview. Just a little one."

Fig reached into his back pocket and pulled out several sheets of paper that had been tri-folded so they could fit in a business envelope.

"Are you Scott Thomas Findle?"

"What?"

"I have to ask. It's a formality. Work with me. Are you Scott Thomas Findle?"

"You know I am, Fig."

"Good," he said. "Here."

"What's this?"

"You've been served," Fig said. "Szczesny is suing you for libel. Over the terrorist thing."

Scott stared at Fig.

"Don't worry," Fig said. "It won't stick. Believe me. I've been sued like 20 times. How many is this for you, Scott?"

"I've never been sued," Scott said meekly. "Over anything."

"No?" Fig asked, surprised. "Well, you always remember your first time."

CHAPTER THIRTEEN

Scott never had an imaginary friend, but his son Ryan did. His name was Jackson. They would play for hours, Ryan and Jackson, pushing fire engines across the floor of Ryan's bedroom, stacking Lincoln logs and building forts out of the furniture. Naturally Jackson spent a lot of time with the family, so for a six-month span, Scott, Felisha and Ryan grew accustomed to buckling Jackson safely into the car, holding doors open for him, pouring him a glass of water at the dinner table, and tucking him in on those nights when he slept over. It was a phase, and Ryan outgrew it quickly when he began school and fostered friendships with actual people. Good thing, too, because as enlightened and tolerant as Scott tried to be, he was losing his patience with the pantomimes.

Scott hadn't thought about Jackson for years, but now he was trying to remember as much as he could about the figment of Ryan's imagination. Particularly he wanted to remember how Ryan acted around Jackson. The nuances. The details. Scott needed an imaginary friend for the night.

From the moment he called Felisha back and agreed to meet her before heading to Chicago and Game Seven, he decided that he would pretend to be on a date with another woman. Jessica. Because why not Jessica?

His mind needed a backstory. He quickly seized on the nurse in Florida who had helped him after The Professor's incident. *Good*, he thought. *We start going out after that. Things get serious. We get engaged, even. Yeah, engaged.*

Jessica would accompany him throughout the evening. Wherever the night would take them. That, he figured, would put the brakes on any temptations he was pretty sure but not absolutely certain he could avoid. He couldn't very well tell Jessica that he was going out for drinks with his ex-wife on what was supposed to be the night before their wedding.

The wedding is tomorrow? Scott jumped, startled by his own imagination, before realizing he was only deep in his own creative process. *Right. Tomorrow. That's what we planned, the day after the season ended.*

So when he showed up to Magoon's, he held the door open for Imaginary Jessica. When he went to the bar, he pulled out a stool for her. When he ordered a beer for himself, he also ordered a glass of chardonnay for Jessica and set it in front of her. He didn't even look at the tip-inducing cleavage the bartender kept flashing, out of respect for the imaginary love of his life who was imaginarily sitting right beside him. Well, he did steal a peek. But he didn't stare. That would be insulting to Jessica.

He tried to imagine her hair, her smell, her polite laugh compared to her actual laugh. Scott was pretty sure he could tell the difference, although there were times when he wasn't sure which he was getting.

Waiting for Felisha, standing with his arm casually draped around the back of the empty barstool, Scott quickly realized his tactical mistake in planning the meeting. He'd wanted to avoid any hint of couplehood with Felisha, so meals were out. Nothing quiet and cozy. Nothing with candles. Scott quickly looked around the bar. *Good*, he thought, *no candles*. But there was something that he didn't consider at Magoon's when he made the suggestion, and only now was he realizing the pitfall. Only now, as he strained to hear what the busty bartender was saying, did he realize just how loud the music was.

That's when Felisha walked in.

And sat down.

Right in Jessica's lap.

"That's not for you," Scott said, trailing off so as not to appear crazy. Just as with Jessica's laugh, though, he was having a hard time telling the difference lately.

Felisha barely made out the words over the din and assumed he'd said "That's for you" and smiled, lifted the glass of wine and sipped it. A streak of red lipstick stuck to the goblet. Scott stared at the lip imprint and swallowed. He didn't know much about makeup, but he assumed that if the lipstick had come off on the glass, that meant it had only recently been applied. And if Felisha had only recently applied the lipstick, then ...

"Thanks!" she smiled. "Chardonnay?"

"Huh?"

Felisha leaned in closer and spoke loudly, right into Scott's ear. *This damn music*, Scott thought as he smelled her.

"Chardonnay?"

Scott pulled back so Felisha could see him nod. Felisha re-entered his halo for further comment.

"I usually don't drink chardonnay," she said. "It's not for me."

The studio audience for Scott's inner monologue giggled.

Felisha took another sip of the white wine, pressing her lips to the exact same spot so as to leave one identical print, only darker and more defined. She was always precise, Scott thought. Then she leaned in again. Scott flinched. He turned his head toward the restrooms, hoping Jessica would be coming out from her brief visit to powder her imaginary nose any moment. Then he turned back to Felisha.

"They used to write songs like this all the time," Felisha said.

"No they didn't," Scott said, insistent on being a contrarian without even fully understanding the topic. "Like what?"

"Songs that had something to say."

He listened to a few bars of Credence singing about senators' sons and star-spangled eyes.

"I doubt your boss appreciates the message," Scott finally said.

"Probably not," Felisha smiled.

"He actually is one, right? A senator's son?"

Felisha nodded at the realization of lyrics imitating life. "Congressman, actually," she said. "Just a two-term rep." For the third time, she sipped the wine she said she did not enjoy.

"That's pretty funny," Scott admitted.

"I guess I meant that they don't write songs like this anymore," Felisha said, their conversation taking place between dips and swoops toward each other's aural canals so as to be heard above the music they were dissecting. It reminded Scott of their first awkward kiss, that pump-fake lean-in the night of the party where they had met. It was loud there, too. They seemed not to mind as much then.

"There are a lot of things they don't do anymore," Scott said, trying to wring as much symbolism as he could from the statement. None of it dripped on Felisha.

Felisha put the wine glass firmly on the bar and squared herself to Scott, who was trying desperately to imagine Jessica as part of the conversation.

"So, I saw you called," Felisha said.

"Yeah, well, I think I pressed the wrong button," Scott stammered, looking to his right, where Imaginary Jessica was standing with her arms crossed and her unhappy foot tapping. "Fig," he added. "Fig called. From my phone, but it was Fig."

"Oh," Felisha said. "What did he want?"

"I don't know," Scott said. "You know Figgy."

He called him Figgy now out of convenience. Felisha nodded.

"I thought maybe you wanted to talk about my offer," she said, and before he could offer his rebuttal, Felisha added: "And don't say 'What offer?' "

Scott nodded as if he'd lost a pawn. He decided to change tactics. To become the aggressor.

"Are you going back to Chicago?" he asked.

"Of course," Felisha said.

"Good," Scott said. "I mean, of course. Why wouldn't you? Especially with another week."

"It hurts us," Felisha said, retreating from the loss of her own pawn. She hadn't applied the lipstick just outside the bar to talk business. "Especially with Ott making it seem he's the problem-solver, bringing Game Seven back to Chicago. The spoils of war or something."

The trick to getting a good lead off first as a baserunner is to take balanced strides. One foot goes out, the other follows. Side-steps. Always one foot on the ground in case you have to dive back to beat a pickoff attempt. And never, NEVER, get your legs crossed. It's physically impossible to make it back to the bag safely if your left leg is crossing in front of your right leg. There's no push. Only a flop. A good pitcher will watch a runner over his shoulder when he takes his lead and wait for that moment when the legs are crossed, then throw a dart to the base for an easy out.

Scott looked down. Felisha's legs were crossed, literally, but he also recognized that he had her off-balance and she couldn't get back to the base safely. Now was the time to pick her off. He spun and threw the pick-off, one that he had not intended to attempt until the very moment the words came out of his mouth. He'd broken the biggest story in the country and been sued over it in the very same day, had to postpone his imaginary wedding for an impromptu trip to Chicago and was pretty sure he somehow was involved in a conspiracy to derail the election of the next President of the United States. Why not add to the jumble?

"What happened that night?"

Felisha froze. Scott borrowed one of her favorite plays for emphasis.

"And don't say 'What night?' "

Felisha nodded.

"You know the basics," she said somberly, embarrassed.

"I do."

"Do we have to talk about this now? Here?"

Scott nodded. A Springsteen song came on. One of those that sounds upbeat and chipper until you really listen to the lyrics. It was about the good old days at first sound, but really it was about the crappy current days. And the song had been around long enough that the crappy current days The Boss was talking about had become the good old days for most of those who heard the song now.

"I was low," Felisha said. "I was tired and sad and confused and I knew Fig would come over if I called him."

"You knew that."

"He didn't want to at first, Scott. I swear."

"But you talked him into it."

"Yes."

"Because you knew that he couldn't resist you."

"Yes."

"That he always loved you."

"Yes."

"Loved you more than I did in some ways. In a lot of ways."

"Yes."

"That he would do anything to make you happy. To make your pain go away. To please you."

"Yes," she said. "And I feel awful about it."

"So tell me," Scott said, almost in a snarl. He didn't need Imaginary Jessica anymore as he stared blisters into Felisha, a newfound strength bubbling up. "Tell me. And don't leave out the part where you feel just awful about it. Because that's the part I'm looking forward to the most."

"Now?"

"Now."

"I know you'll never forgive me," Felisha began, "but hopefully, knowing this, you'll someday be able to forgive Fig."

It was almost as if she had practiced that preamble for when she would have to come clean, scroungy sordid details and all. But she had one last pawn of Scott's to take out. One last sexy taunt to let him know that she knew him better than anyone. Better than Jessica knew him. Better than he knew himself, even.

"You'd better check your watch," she said.

Scott resisted the temptation, avoiding his wrist as he'd avoided the cleavage behind the bar, opening the aperture of his field of vision to include the coveted object without blatantly focusing on it. Felisha smiled at the struggle.

And with that, she took a deep breath and began the story.

"You'd asked for the divorce and been gone for a week …"

PART THREE

CHAPTER FOURTEEN

Emerson Ott was born at his father's graveside, swaddled in an American flag. You've seen the picture. The one on the cover of LIFE magazine on February 12, 1967. The father, Spc. Thomas James Ott, had been killed in Vietnam 16 days earlier, crushed by a jeep that fell off its jack while he was trying to change a flat tire. Hardly a glorious or heroic passing -- official military inquiries labeled the cause of death "wind" and pinned the demise on the unusually strong gusts recorded in the area -- but it was, in the small town of Franklin, Illinois (just outside of Chicago, where he and his young widowed bride had met, grown up and married) at once devastating and cause for celebration. One of Franklin's own had given his life to the war effort. That he was not killed handling an M-16 or juggling land mines on the way to the front line but with a tire iron in his grip seemed of little consequence.

His wife, the former Penny Lynn Bestfield, was nine months pregnant at the time of his mishap, nine and a half at the funeral attended by the proper dignitaries and escorts appropriate a man of Spc. Thomas James Ott's standing. It was the first military funeral in Franklin since 1919; somehow World War II had managed to fly right over the town.

Soldiers snapped the flag resting over his coffin into a neat

triangle and handed it to his sobbing, swollen wife sitting graveside on a white folding chair. Lt. John Schroeder, the highest
ranking officer at the ceremony, stood briskly to signal the 21-
gun salute accompanying the lowering of the casket.

No one heard Penny Lynn's screams as the first volley of
shots rang out, inducing a labor which, unlike her drawn-out
pregnancy, progressed with startling rapidity. By the second
round of rifle shots, Penny Lynn lay on the frozen ground, her
fingers clenching what little greenery was left of the Greenlawn
Cemetery grass. At the third and final round of explosions, the
child's mouth gasped fresh air.

Quick-thinking Lt. Schroeder holstered his saber, grabbed the
keepsake flag, and eased the new baby into the world, literally
cloaking Emerson Ott in stars and stripes from birth.

The famous photo hit the wires and spread around the
world, quickly adopted both by those opposed to and in support of the war in Vietnam. The peace-lovers cringed and hollered at the image of another fatherless child brought into a
chaotic world filled with armed men in uniforms who snatch
newborns directly from their mothers' wombs to corrupt them
with a blind patriotism. The hawks saluted the black-and-
white image, equating it to the finest vision of the flag since
Francis Scott Key's ... until the World War II veterans
howled at the overlooking of Iwo Jima, creating debate within
debate. Still, those who supported the war generally agreed to
its value, if not its ranking in history. Wasn't this what the
man had died for, so his son could live in the greatest country
in the world, free to choose everything from a president to an
ice cream flavor? That the man's name escaped their minds,
or that he'd be alive if Saigon had a AAA chapter, was not
considered reason to diminish his accomplishment.

But the younger Ott never gave the photo much political weight. As he grew up in Franklin, the treasured snapshot hardly ever left his wallet or his nightstand, where it stood framed (next to only one other picture: that of his great-uncle Melvin Thomas Ott, the Hall of Fame slugger for the Giants). Here was, he realized at an early age, the only complete family photo he would ever have.

He held the middle, the focus, the famous red, white and blue blankie framing his bruised and bloody face, the vivid colors unmistakable despite the grayscale of the print. Mom took the left, her black skirt rolled to her waist, face drawn, the anguish of losing her love and the piercing pain of producing a replacement clearly visible in her eyes. And there, in the right corner, the top of dad's casket could be seen before it disappeared into the ground. The first, last and only time they would all be together had been captured on film and shared with the world.

Each year, February returned to Franklin, Illinois, along with the journalists and sightseers. Emerson Ott would spent 11 months convincing his friends, teachers and even his mother to forget his celebrity, only to have television and newspaper reports destroy his work.

The packs of journalists arrived each year for the anniversary of the famous photograph -- typically a larger group assembled every five years for the "big" anniversaries of 10 and 15 -- to unveil what became of the boy in that photograph and attempt to scrub answers to their own lives' questions.

"What did you think of Nixon's resignation?" a reporter from the Franklin Tribune, who also happened to live three houses down from the Otts and passed Emerson playing in the yard each day but never stopped to even say hello any of those times, asked him on his eighth birthday.

"Do you think we should boycott this summer's Olympics?" another reporter -- this time from an out-of-town paper, likely New York or Washington but probably not Chicago because Chicago papers tended to focus more on personalities than policies-- asked him at age 13.

Emerson Ott never recalled his mother being asked any questions.

February 12 already was a day of import in Illinois, as it marked Abraham Lincoln's birthday. The date held added meaning in Franklin as the town celebrated, at first unofficially and then with great reverence, Emerson Ott Day. Though never formalized as a holiday or noted in any official civic records, Emerson Ott Day -- or Em Day, as it was known in shorthand -- became one of the few successful ventures for the town of Franklin. No one seemed to notice that the celebration actually marked the anniversary of the publication of the photo and not the boy's birth itself.

In 1982, when Emerson was 15, a graveside reenactment of his birth was performed, a sort of living nativity. Penny Lynn, Emerson and the mayor stood on a white gazebo built in the cemetery -- several less-photographed tombs were excavated and moved for the construction project -- and watched as a beautiful young actress screamed, collapsed dramatically to the ground, then yanked a plastic baby from under her black dress to the wild applause of the crowd of 75 or so townsfolk. The only piece of the scene not a prop or stand-in was the headstone of Spc. Thomas James Ott, anchoring center stage.

Penny Lynn reached over and removed the Cubs cap from her son's head for the playing of Taps. When the tribute was over, the mayor slapped Emerson on the back, as an obstetrician might have 15 years earlier had he been born in typical surroundings, then raised the shy teenager's arm as a champion. Penny Lynn, who never fully recovered from the jarring loss of her husband, smiled. It was the only day of the year she smiled, the day she least felt like doing so. She had never embraced the photograph as her son had, she kept no such image in any of the living areas of their home, nor did she carry a wallet-sized shot in her purse. She allowed Emerson his fascination with the photograph, so long as it remained in his bedroom, but Emerson soon came to recognize the times Penny Lynn had been in his room either delivering laundry or tidying or just snooping. He could tell because the framed photograph on his dresser was placed facedown. Never disrespected, just gently and convincingly reposed.

When Emerson Ott left home on his 20th birthday -- barely a week prior to the biggest Em Day festivities yet -- few were truly surprised, nor were they tremendously disappointed. The celebration went on without him, Penny Lynn standing on the fading white gazebo steps apologizing for Emerson's absence but speaking for him in thanking all of the people who'd shown up to help make the day so special. There were 45 of them gathered in the cemetery, a smaller crowd than usual because of the light snow that was falling. The mayor -- a different mayor from the one who'd overseen the 15 year-celebration; he was buried just beyond the gazebo by then -- presented Penny Lynn a citation for her collection, and on the way home, she brought it to the Emerson Ott store on North Morton Street, where it was put on display with the other 16 (there had been three years when weather had canceled the celebration) and the original placenta-stained American flag.

The following year, an actor was hired to portray Emerson at the ceremony. The Franklin Tribune did not note the understudy, not even in captioning the photograph of Penny Lynn Ott kissing him politely on the cheek.

Ott may have left Franklin, but he never left Illinois. He quickly rose through Chicago politics, becoming a congressman, and eventually a senator. While his background was well-known, his history time-capsuled in a way few others have their life documented, he considered himself a son of Chicago.

That son was now bringing Game Seven home with him.

It was the most agreeable November day that anyone in Chicago could remember. A Cubs-blue sky dapped with luscious white clouds. The sun shone brightly, and because of its angle in the sky due to the lateness of the year, it cast gorgeous shadows throughout the city. In no place were those contrasts between light and dark more appreciated than at Wrigley Field, when Game Seven was hours away from commencement.

The building hadn't been expecting to host another event that year, never mind one of this magnitude, but it was up to the challenge. There were some obstacles. The spaceship-like structure that was going to be fitted atop the roof was in pieces on the streets outside the ballpark awaiting a winter of assembly, creating some traffic issues. Most of the vendors during the summer were part-time seasonal workers and not all of them could be called back into service on such short notice, so the anticipation was for longer-than-usual lines at the concession stands.

But on the field that afternoon, everything was sublime. As the Cubs took batting practice, their infielders gobbled up ground balls and their outfielders and non-starting pitchers were sprayed across the outfield shagging flies, Scott stood against the railing of the Red Sox dugout chatting with Niles Weilander, the starting pitcher from Game Five, who would be used only in a bullpen emergency. Daryl Hoyt, the Boston starter for Game Seven, skipped up the steps next to them, gave Niles a pat on the rear, and headed out for a light pre-game jog around the warning track.

Scott thought about the late Buster Sinclair; it was hard not to as he started out toward left field. He thought about Ryan, with whom he had been able to exchange only brief FaceTime conversations and texts but no real conversations. He didn't think about the libel suit, which JKL had assured him would be dismissed. Nor did he think about Felisha. Fig? Well, Fig was off doing something Figgish, he assumed.

Somewhere in his shriveled sportswriter soul, as wrinkled as his wardrobe, he believed it had been worth the wait to be able to witness this spectacle.

Everyone seemed to be on the same plane.

Behind the batting cage, The Commissioner and Roger Fleiss were sharing a light-hearted moment. With the election postponed, not only were they the only live programming for the night but they had taken on an extra $15 million in political advertising for the game.

In front of the Cubs' dugout, Ott was addressing another bank of cameras and microphones, giddily thundering away about the Cubs and no doubt taking credit again for bringing the game back to Chicago.

At the end of the Red Sox's dugout, closer to home plate than where Scott and Niles were perched, Brandt was talking casually with his political comrade, Dan Wick, the mayor of Chicago. Not only did they share political views, but on this night they shared baseball interests. Wick was the most high-profile fan of the White Sox in the city, and he wore his black Sox cap that night at Wrigley as if he were in fact a villain from a Western movie, daring any gunslinger in the saloon to make him take it off. The two men watched Ott's performance from afar, smiling and pointing.

Everyone was relaxed. Everyone was happy. The only divisions were good-natured ones. Baseball, Scott thought, had done this. Only baseball was capable of bringing people together on such a night, allowing them to dismiss their troubles and forget their differences and enjoy life with a cold beer and bag of peanuts. The game was set to start at 7:20 p.m. local time. Nothing could stop it, from what Scott could see. Not a dead outfielder, not a freak snowstorm, not a non-terrorist attack with a wrecking ball, not a presidential election.

"Isn't this great?" Scott said wistfully to Niles, their elbows slung back over the padded railing. "What a day for baseball, huh? What a sky!"

Niles looked up.

"Getting a little dark," he noted.

Scott noticed that too.

"It's called ambience," he said with a true smile. "I'm sure the lights will come on soon."

And God saw the light, and it was good; and God divided the light from the darkness.

That happened, as it says vaguely but emphatically a few sentences earlier, "in the beginning." The beginning of what, it never makes certain. Everything, it is supposed. That's a long time ago.

But it wasn't until 1988 that the City of Chicago decided to divide the light from the darkness and allow the installation of electric luminescence at Wrigley Field.

Wrigley was the last of the big league stadiums to be without lights, and in 1983, the Chicago City Council enacted an ordinance that banned night athletic contests in any playing field that is not totally enclosed, has more than 15,000 seats and is within 500 feet of 100 dwelling units. It just so happened that there was only one place in the city that fit such a description. So when the

Cubs won the division in 1984 and earned the right to have homefield advantage over the Padres in a best-of-five NLCS, they were prohibited from playing night games. That resulted in some creative scheduling by the league, which already was hitched to primetime baseball games on television. Instead of the final three games of the series, the Cubs got to host the first two. They won both. But then they went to San Diego and lost three in a row in Southern California. If Wrigley Field had lights, the Cubs would have played three games in their home whites with thin blue pinstripes instead of just two. Who knows how that would have affected the outcome?

Eventually, the Council voted to allow the erection of lights atop the stadium and the playing of a very select number of night games. Because of the battle between residents and the team, the parameters that enclosed the use of the lights were very specific and very strict. For example, only 18 night games were allowed per season. There could not be night games on successive dates. The public address system had to be turned down to a certain decibel level so as not to add noise pollution to the light pollution.

Most of those details still were on the books, but they were largely ignored as night baseball at Wrigley became more and more common. By 2010 there were entire homestands of night games complete with the loud, thundering sound effects and product placements that accompanied every major-league game of the day. The three Cubs home games of the current World Series were all played long after the sun had dropped below the horizon.

One of those arcane limitations that was overlooked but still existed in stealthy and official legislative code was Ordinance 246.73.ii(j). It was added to the rules in the '80s as an afterthought to prevent Wrigley Field from hosting offseason concerts or other events that would disrupt the neighborhood. Specifically, it allowed the use of the lights only from April 1 through October 31. At the time, no one could envision three layers of seven-game playoff series pushing a World Series game into November.

It wasn't until the Cubs had finished their batting practice and the Red Sox were stretching on the grass in front of their dugout that Scott began to worry about the encroaching night. But he didn't leave his post. He kept looking up at the stanchions, figuring that the bulbs would begin to flicker at any time.

They never did.

"The law is the law," Mayor Wick told reporters, standing on the dark infield of Wrigley illuminated only by a halo of camera lights. "I took an oath to uphold it. Without law, there is nothing but anarchy."

"Not even America's pastime should be above America's governance," Brandt added, enjoying having stolen the narrative from Ott. "When I'm elected president, I'll be sure that all of my policies fall within the law of the land. Unlike my opponent, who seems to believe he can skirt the rules and ignore the will of the people."

The players and politicians and fans and officials and vendors and groundskeepers had all left. Scott remained, arms reaching back over the railing on that dugout fence, staring at the lamps. Those dark, flatlined lamps. He'd missed deadline. He hadn't written a word. He just kept trying to will those big bulbs to life.

Finally, at about 10 o'clock or so, Fig found him in near catatonic shock.

"You ever see that movie 'The Natural?'" Scott asked Fig in a voice just above a whisper.

"Sure. A bunch of times I guess."

"What's your favorite scene?"

"Most people, I'd suspect, would say when the home run crashes into the lights at the end," Fig said, "but I love the beginning. When he strikes out that guy. That big guy on the train. What's his name?"

"The Whammer," Scott said without hesitating.

"Right. The Whammer. He strikes him out and pumps his fist into his hand."

"Great scene," Scott said. "Ask me mine."

"OK," Fig played along, "what's your favorite scene?"

"It's just a line, really," Scott said. "Toward the end. Robert Redford is in the hospital and Glenn Close comes to visit him and he's sitting on the edge of the bed and they're talking about their lives and their childhood together and the paths they've taken."

"I remember it," Fig said. "I think. It's a maternity ward or something, isn't it?"

Scott nodded.

"Redford is sitting on the edge of the bed and he stares off into space," Scott said. "And he delivers this line, not really to Glenn Close but more to himself. He says it just loud enough to be heard. Just like I'm talking to you now. You have to re-watch the movie a couple of times to catch it, I didn't notice it myself, but it's the most important line in the film."

"What's he say?"

"He says, *God, I love baseball.*"

They stared at the darkened infield.

"Just like that," Scott said. "Just a quick, heart-felt declaration, but he doesn't have to shout it. It's quiet. And it's being taken away from him. *God, I love baseball.*"

They stared some more.

"Guess I'll have to go back and watch it again," Fig said.

"When this is over."

"They broke me tonight," Scott mumbled.

"They?" Fig asked.

"The politicians. The owners. The networks. The editors and deadlines. Felisha. You. The bullshit. The powers pulling without thinking. I had it my mind, Fig, that this was about baseball. It's not. Baseball isn't about baseball anymore. How ridiculous does that sound?"

"Pretty ridiculous," Fig said patiently, as if humoring a drinking buddy.

"And you know what? I hate it. I fucking hate it. All of it. I've been standing here for hours staring at those lamps and they won't turn on and I've been thinking about it and I just have to say it, Fig. I have to say it. I hate baseball."

"You don't hate baseball."

"I do. I fucking hate it."

"You can't hate baseball. Baseball is who you are. That'd be like hating yourself."

Scott looked away from the unlit lights and at Fig.

"I guess so."

"Come on," Fig said, his arm around Scott's shoulder, guiding him gently back through the dugout to leave the stadium. "It's closing time."

Scott took a few steps with Fig, then broke away, sprinted up the steps, ran onto the field, charged up the mound. He emptied his pockets, flinging pens and notebooks and digital recorders and even his iPhone across the infield. When he was out of projectiles, he started wildly swinging his arms.

"I HATE YOU!" he was screaming all the while, his words echoing through the dark, empty seats. "I HATE YOU! I HATE YOU! I FUCKING HATE YOU!"

CHAPTER FIFTEEN

Had the Cubs made the World Series in 1985, the first year baseball decided all World Series games would be played at night, they would have hosted their share of the games at Busch Stadium in St. Louis. The Cubs being the Cubs in 1985, it never came to that. Now, three decades later, with Mayor Wick dug into his no-lights foxhole, unwilling to budge over the matter, and the weight of Governor Brandt's presidential campaign behind him, the Cubs again were in need of a postseason home away from home. This time, the hunt required more urgency.

Baseball, it seemed, had little input in the decision. The Commissioner offered up idea after idea, none of which was suitable to any or all parties involved.

The first thought was to simply move the game across town to the home of the White Sox. Ott was in favor of that. It would keep the game in Chicago, at least. But Brandt and Wick opposed it. Wick quickly signed a mayoral order giving the White Sox a grant of $10 million in city money for the resodding of their field, provided that work began on the project immediately. "Shovel-ready" programs, they were called. By the time baseball executives reached ComSky Park – named after the communications satellite company and a cute play against the original Comisky name -- to scout out its readiness, there weren't shovels but bulldozers on the infield tearing up the old grass.

It eventually was determined -- by someone, somewhere, though who and where was never made clear -- that Game Seven should be played at a neutral stadium. That ruled out cities where either of the two teams were particularly appreciated or despised. New York, St. Louis, Milwaukee, Tampa. Phoenix was briefly considered, but the Red Sox objected that it was too close to the Cubs' spring training home.

With the wrath of November bearing down on most of the northern part of the country and an overdue presidential election that was dividing the nation, the game had to find the proper climate, both meteorological and political.

Miami. It was a National League park, which was somewhat beneficial to the Cubs. It was far enough away from the Red Sox's spring training home, but still driveable for any snowbird fans who might want to make the trip across the state. The Cubs objected to that at first, but the Red Sox argued that they were supposed to host Game Seven anyway.

Miami on Thursday. It was settled.

"You still broken?" Fig asked Scott at the gate.

"Probably," Scott said.

He didn't look it anymore. Wasn't acting it either. He seemed to be the same old Scott, calmed down from the previous night's tantrum, during which he'd said things that he felt he should regret... but didn't.

"I guess we all are, to some degree," Fig said.

Scott, Fig and The Professor were 35,000 feet above someplace between Chicago and Miami when they received the email that the game would not be played in Miami. Brandt and Ott had publicly wagered the total number of electorate votes from the swing state of Florida on the outcome of the game, a maneuver that even the District Attorney of the Sunshine State found reprehensible. She put the kibosh on any baseball game played in the state that would deflate Florida's already uninspiring reputation for voter accuracy and integrity.

When the trio landed at Miami International Airport, they immediately searched out the customer service representative and booked the next flight to where the game now was scheduled to be played.

They barely had time to hit the men's room in Miami before they were back in the air heading west. To San Diego.

When they went to sleep that night in San Diego, they still believed in the possibility. But when Scott awoke the next morning, a Friday, and turned the television on to CNN, he was not entirely surprised to learn that a glitch had mucked up the plans once again.

Live shots of the San Diego airport showed a large jet on the runway surrounded by hundreds of people standing shoulder to shoulder. Brandt had become part of the Red Sox's traveling party -- or vice versa, it may have been -- and when word spread that he was arriving in San Diego on the team plane that morning, immigration reform activists quickly mobilized to send him a message. Brandt had not even bothered to do much campaigning in California and certainly never ventured into the southern part of the state, but one of the planks of his platform was the construction of a wall along the border to keep illegals in Mexico.

"We want to show Governor Brandt how dehumanizing it is to be walled up," one of the protestors told the CNN correspondent on the tarmac. "We've built this Wall of Dignity, a Wall of the Human Spirit, to keep him out of San Diego until he agrees to abandon his plans for a similar wall just a few miles from here."

Scott's phone buzzed.

"You watching this?" Fig asked.

"Yeah."

"Felisha just called me," Fig said. "She said they can't get off the plane. Not the team. Not Brandt. No one."

"Why don't they call in the authorities? Get those people out of there?"

"There's no money," Fig said. "California is broke. They can't pay the National Guard to do it. They spent all of their money putting up and taking down the polling stations on Tuesday for the election that wasn't."

"Isn't that perfect," Scott said. "Hang on, let me turn the TV down. The plane is revving its engines and I can barely hear you."

Scott adjusted the volume, buried the indicator all the way at zero, and hit the mute button for good measure. He still heard the plane. Then he squinted at the television screen.

"Fig, where are you?"

"At the airport!" he screamed.

"Next to the guy in green holding the sign that says 'The Only Wall the Red Sox Should Back Is At Fenway'?"

Fig looked up and read the sign.

"Yeah!" he hollered. "Can you see me?"

Fig began waving that awkward wave of someone who realizes he is on television but cannot do the proper computations to figure out where the camera is. As Scott watched him, he appeared to be flagging down someone standing in front of the door in his hotel room.

"I see you," Scott said. "Please, for the love of God, stop waving."

"Watch this!" Fig shouted, then pulled the phone away from his ear and began thrusting his fist in the air rhythmically. *No ball, no wall!* he began chanting. *No ball, no wall!* Soon the entire chain link of demonstrators had picked up on his little couplet. Fig brought the phone back to the side of his head. "Do you hear that, Scott? I'm a natural at this!"

"It doesn't even make sense," Scott said, frustrated. "It makes it sound like you want the wall."

"What?"

"Like you want," he said loudly and slowly, "the wall."

"I'm having too much fun," Fig said. "I'll call you back."

By the time he did, the plane carrying the Red Sox and Brandt and Felisha had taken off and headed back to Boston. The Cubs, meanwhile, boarded their plane and returned to Chicago. The World Series was in a stalemate.

The Professor, whose post-retirement enthusiasm for the adventure they were undertaking had deteriorated to the point of near constant-whining and complaining, gave up too.

"I'm heading home," he said as he left San Diego for his home in Florida. "See you in spring training, Scott. If there is one. Good luck."

It was just as well. JKL had called the night before. The travel budget was taking a beating. If things didn't get resolved soon – and by resolved, JKL meant a Game Seven – he was going to have to cut the entourage from three to two. The Professor said he wanted to stay on board just to drain the last few beans from JKL's count, but he didn't have the stomach for such spite.

That left Scott and Fig sitting in the lobby of the San Diego hotel that night staring blankly at The Commissioner and Sy Galoosh. They had no place else to go. There were no other immediate options in front of them.

"I thought this was going to be it," The Commissioner muttered. "San Diego. Laid back. Great weather. What could go wrong?"

"We'll think of something," Galoosh said.

"This can't be the first season to finish without a champion since the 1994 strike," The Commissioner said.

"Wait," Fig interjected, "you're giving up?"

"We're out of options," Galoosh sighed. "We can't play the game on Saturday or Sunday because of the network's football commitments. We can't find a location that anyone can agree upon. What else can we do?"

Scott began to allow the reality to roll over him like the gentle Pacific waves in the paintings of the hotel lobby. No World Series champion? That would be terrible. But at least it would be over. He could go home. See Ryan. End the season. Get a lawyer.

Maybe it wasn't so terrible.

The country already started to move past the idea of the World Series anyway. Football season was heating up. Hockey season and the NBA were starting. Thanksgiving was just three weeks away, for God's sake. For how much longer could this go on?

Scott's thoughts were interrupted by the crassly digitized notes of "La Cucaracha." He looked around to spot the source of the noise and stared into Fig's eyes.

"Oh," Fig said. "That's me."

He pulled out his phone and looked at the screen. Scott looked at The Commissioner and Galoosh, both clearly less acclimated to Fig's eccentricities. Scott had built up something of a tolerance to them over the years.

"This is the call I've been waiting for," he said. "Excuse me, fellas. I'll be back in about 20 minutes and I may have a solution to your problem."

Fig rose from his chair and answered the phone as he began to walk away from the group of men who were stranded both physically and mentally.

"*El Presidente*," Fig said into the phone as he searched for a secluded area to hold his conversation. "So *bueno* to hear from you again, *por favor!*"

CHAPTER SIXTEEN

Ten pitches.

That was the tryout. He didn't even get a chance to warm up from the mound. He and the others could only toss baseballs around the infield, estimating the distance of 60 feet and six inches, to get their arms limber and their mechanics fine-tuned.

Major league teams were intent on staying in business throughout World War II, even though the crop of healthy, athletic 18- to 30-year-olds that they usually harvested for their rosters was being put to use in Germany, Italy, North Africa and the Pacific. Future Hall of Fame players such as Ted Williams, Joe DiMaggio, Yogi Berra and Bob Feller interrupted their careers to serve in the military during that time, which left their teams scrounging for talent. To fill the void, many teams resorted to open tryouts such as these, where hundreds of professional baseball hopefuls filled a stadium and had a handful of seconds to impress a scout or a coach with their particular skill.

"OK," he was told. "Next."

It reminded him of his uncle's barber shop back home. Most of the children in his neighborhood could not afford a proper trim of their hair, their mamas or papas doing the best they could with whatever sharp cutting instruments were available. He would have been among that group, too. The illegitimate son of a farmer, he grew up poor. His uncle -- illegitimate uncle -- was poor, too. But his skill was shearing and shaving, and the wealthy on the small island would come to him for their weekly treatments. Uncle would ease the men back so they were horizontal in the big red chair; as a child, he was small enough and on the floor often enough to look at the steel gears and clamps below the chair that created the levitation above, admiring the blind footwork Uncle danced to get the customer into just the right position. From there Uncle would lather the face, usually working around the thick stump of a cigar that remained puckered in the patient's mouth, and slowly, delicately, precisely begin to carve the whiskers from the man's face.

He could hear the steel scraping the coarse sandpaper faces smooth, smell the fragrances of the lotions that were applied afterward to soothe the work. A final coat of varnish. Then more footwork to bring the chair erect, and then those steady hands that had moments earlier guided sharp metal just millimeters of skin away from the jugular came to life, quaking and flicking and pinching the scissors between the thumb and the middle finger like a castanet.

Ch-ch-ch-ch-ch. Ch-ch-ch-ch-ch.

The rhythm of the hands matched by the spray of falling hairs that floated to the ground. Then the soft-bristled broom across the neck. Then the talc applied in a puff that mingled with the haze of the cigar smoke. And finally, one last toe-tap to lower the seat and the removal of the linen covering that Uncle would flick and snap, a magician proudly revealing his trick.

"*Proximo!*" he would say as he matadored the cape in his hand and escorted the now-tamed bull from the seat and made room for the next charging bearded beast. Once a month, the boy was next, and on the word -- *Proximo!* -- he would bound into the chair. There were no hairs on his calf cheeks to shear, but the hot foam was applied and removed and the eye-stinging coolants splashed on him. His head was properly sculpted, and he could hear up close not only the tapping of the castanets but the slight squeak that the perpetually moving scissors created as they pinched and released, sliced and cast, shaped and shorn. He was always sad when he had to come down off that chair, the magic carpet ride having ended, the flick of the cape creating the snap of a hypnotist bringing him out of his slumber. *Proximo*!

"Let's go," the coach said again. "Next!"

He climbed the mound at Yankee Stadium the way he did that chair, walking around it first before backing up from the front. He looked at the empty seats and imagined them filled with thousands of people chanting his name and holding signs in honor of him. He'd been a decent pitcher in his hometown of Santiago, not a power thrower with an overwhelming fastball that he could buzz past all the hitters, but a crafty tactician who was more a survivor than a dominator. He relied on his defense and had an uncanny knack for getting a ground ball whenever his team needed a double play. Those were not the kinds of things that would show up in 10 pitches. It takes time to observe those skills. Several games, at least, to appreciate them.

"Let's go!" one of the coaches yelled to him as he scanned the empty seats. "Ten pitches. Or three minutes. Whichever comes first."

He nodded and turned his attention to the catcher behind the plate. With his feet on the rubber, he hunched over ever so slightly and stared at the glove before beginning his windup. He swung his arms behind him to gain momentum, then brought them forward over his head, reaching back as if he were about to tag second base. His left foot stepped back and his whole body hung, a horizontal picture frame hooked to the pitcher's rubber by the metal cleat under the toe of his right foot. Once fully elasticized, he began the journey forward. The left leg kicked high in the air, his torso twisted and he briefly hid his lightly bearded face in the crook of his left shoulder. Then came the explosion. Driving forth on his right leg. Straightening his body toward the target so he was square-chested with home plate in battle-ready position. The left leg, the one that had gone skyward, leaped toward the batter's box and the right arm followed, releasing the baseball just as the appendage began to cross over that square chest.

It felt good out of his hand, but when he saw the catcher leap up from his squat to try to snag the ball as it sailed over his head, he realized it was high. Too high. It zoomed all the way to the stands, snapping sharply against the wood seats behind home plate. He stood in disbelief, gave a non-verbal apology to his catcher, and caught another baseball from the coaches who were standing between third base and the pitcher's mound for their evaluations.

"Nine more," the coach said drearily.

The rest of the pitches were better -- if not in, then at least close to the strike zone. The last two had been curveballs that he snapped off and spun into the catcher's mitt for what would have been strikes.

"What did you get?" the coach yelled to the scout sitting in the stands, just a few seats from the one that the first pitch had thwacked.

"Seventy-nine!" he yelled back without looking up from the clipboard on which he was writing notes and numbers. The coaches nodded at each other.

"OK," the one yelled, "thank you. Next."

Proximo.

He was not meant to be a baseball player. At least not professionally. Not in the United States. So he returned home and en-
rolled in law school at the University of Havana, where he began
to develop an anti-imperialistic temperament thanks to the U.S.-
backed government's unfair treatment of his Uncle... and maybe
the spurn from the Yankees. Eventually, he led a revolution. The
Revolution.

That was a lifetime ago. He no longer was the dictator of Cuba;
he'd stepped back from those responsibilities years ago, yielding
to his brother. Now he was a sick, dying old man whose policies
were as antiquated and feeble as he had become.

But he still loved baseball. Still thought often of those 10
pitches from the crown of the hill at Yankee Stadium. Still believed that, if given more of an opportunity, he might have made
it in the sport.

He followed the game closely and was keenly aware of the
situation regarding the American World Series when he received
a text message. The content of the note was brief.

*FC: Need stadium 4 Gm7 of WS. 1st pitch urs if can play in
Cuba. Call back. Fig*

Even at his advanced age, he was sure he would be able to am-
ble to the top of that mound in the middle of the otherwise level
playing field, the only area in any sport that is elevated above the
rest -- a stage, really -- and recapture his pitching motion. Throw a
strike on the first pitch, unlike almost 70 years earlier. Avenge the
wild pitch that haunted him, the one that, he sometimes considered
in periods of self-reflection and analysis, might just have led him to
become so angry and disenchanted with authority.

And what better Screw You would there be than, as one of his
final acts on this Earth, to have the jewel of American sports and

culture, the most important baseball game in the last 100 years, played on Cuban soil?

He called back.

"Cuba?" The Commissioner gasped when Fig returned to the San Diego hotel lobby with an agreement in principle to hold Game Seven of the World Series at *Estadio Latinoamericano* in Havana. "Can we do that?"

"Well, we can," Galoosh told The Commissioner.

"We can!" he said, leaping from his seat at his old man speed that first involved a rock back to bring all of him out of the cushion when he got moving forward, then a steadying once on his feet, knees bent like an Olympic power lifter, before straightening his legs to reach the fullness of primate evolution. "Yes!" he said, pumping a fist as part of the standing process.

"Technically," Galoosh said. "Technically we can. We have -- you have that is -- the authority to act in the best interest of baseball on any matter. But in reality, we can't."

"We can't?" The Commissioner whined, his mood changing much more quickly than his posture. He plopped back into the chair, gravity now his ally, in a fraction of the time it took him to push his way out of it, landing with a ploompf.

"Well," Galoosh added quickly, "we'd have to clear it with the State Department and other officials. There isn't time."

Relations with Cuba had begun to thaw in recent years. Policies that had stood for a half century were being reversed. Trade and travel were allowed. But then came the "Spring Break Riots." And the arrests of the drunk, half-naked college students. And the burning of Señor Frog's. The obnoxious Americans were too much for the long-sheltered Cuban people. They were expelled, the border and coastline were closed, and no Americans were allowed back, this time by order of the Cuban government and not the U.S. State Department. The construction of a wall was debated.

Baseball, though, could rebuild the bridge.

"What other options do you have right now?" Fig said, sliding his chair across the carpet and swinging it so the four men huddled, leaning forward, talking in hushed tones. If they were meeting on a baseball diamond, whoever was speaking would have put a glove over his mouth to prevent the opponent from lip-reading any strategic secrets. "Think about it."

"He's right," Scott piped up. "There really are no other options."

"But ... Cuba?" The Commissioner reiterated.

"It'll be fine," Fig said. "He's really excited."

"We don't even know what the weather is like there," Galoosh said. "What condition the stadium is in."

"It's great," Fig said. "I mean, I've never been there. But I've always wanted to go. I guess it's a Hemingway thing. I'm sure it's fine."

"There are a lot of questions," Galoosh said, not the least of which should have been how Fig and El Presidente had become pals, but that went unasked for the sake of urgency. It was simply accepted that if there were one person in America -- the world, perhaps -- who would have the number of the former dictator of Cuba programmed into his cellphone to the point that it even had its own identifying ringtone, it would be Fig O'Leary. "We'll have to run it past a few sets of eyes and ears. I'm not sure how the network will feel about it."

"They'll love it," Scott said, representing, he felt, the journalism sector. "Who wouldn't tune in to see a game in Cuba, land of mystery and enchantment behind a door that has been closed to us since the 1960s."

Galoosh nodded.

"This might just work," The Commissioner said.

"Listen, don't tell anyone about it," Galoosh said to Scott and Fig. "I don't want to get burned on another failed attempt to play this game."

"OK," Scott said quickly.

"Uh, yeah," Fig muttered. "It might be a little too late for that." Galoosh's phone began to shimmy with texts and emails from reporters around the country trying to confirm Fig's story, which had just been published on the website.

"You wrote it already?" Galoosh said.

"I wrote it earlier this morning," Fig said. "I just sent it in a few minutes ago. I wanted to talk to Señor Seamhead first. He's a real nut. Loves the game. Hates the Yankees but loves the game. More than Scotty. You guys would really love to sit back with a few mojitos and cigars and talk some beisbol, Scott."

"Maybe," Scott said. "After this is all over."

"So," Fig said, "now that that's settled ... How does one get from San Diego to Havana?"

"I don't know," Scott said, "I think you have to go through Canada."

CHAPTER SEVENTEEN

The Honeymoon Suite at the Marriott on the Canadian side offered a knee-buckling view into the bowl of the Falls. At night,
colorful strobes illuminated the cascading water as it plunged
over some of the most awe-inspiring views that Nature had ever
seen fit to design.

When Scott first walked into the room, it was dark outside,
the curtains were drawn and the lights in the room were off. He
felt as if he were tumbling over the lip of the majestic crescent as
he stepped toward the window. There were a few drops of water-
fall splatter that had accumulated on the outside sill, even from
this far away and this far up, demonstrating the force the rushing
river was generating.

Scott moved close to the window, nearly touching it with his
nose, staring at Niagara, hardly able to breathe. In all of his trav-
els, he'd become accustomed to disappointments as a tourist.
The tower in Chicago wasn't really that much bigger than the
ones in other cities. The monuments in Washington were pretty
small, really. The California beaches were crowded. Even the
Anchor Bar in Buffalo earlier that evening was a flop. Few sights
were able to live up to their billing, especially when a professional cynic was doing the seeing.

But this.

"My God," Scott said in a hushed tone. Something about the raw power, the never-ending flow, the fact that it was just ... there. That no one had planned it or placed it or plopped it down. That people came to see it and nothing else for hundreds of miles. That it didn't need signs or gimmicks to draw your attention to it. It wasn't even the biggest in the world.

"Would you look at that."

Click.

The lights came on in the room and suddenly all Scott could see was his own reflection in the glass of the window. The Falls were still out there, but some of the magic was lost. With the lights on, Scott could see the wires that held up the levitating woman. He could spot the coin that was supposed to be hidden behind the hand, pinched between the fore and middle fingers until it was time to pull it out from behind his ear.

It had been several years since Scott had been in position to appreciate -- or regret -- the house lights coming up in a bar at closing time. One minute you're sitting in dusky delusion, unable to make out the depressing details that surround you. The next, you realize you are sitting in a puddle of some kind, not of your own making, and the echoes of the jukebox are still ringing in your ears when the mop boy comes by to swipe away whatever it is you are in the middle of.

"Why'd you turn the lights on?" Scott said, turning around.

"Because it was dark," Fig said.

Scott shook his head in disgust.

It had been six days since they'd left Boston bound for Chicago, planning to cover Game Seven of the World Series. It had been two weeks since Scott and Fig were thrust together, forced to re-establish a civilized working relationship at the very least. Scott had not gotten back together with Felisha. He missed his son. He missed baseball, and hated having to cover the business of it rather than the beauty of it. The lights in that room had been flicked on, too.

He'd traveled from Chicago to Miami to San Diego to New York and here, to Niagara Falls, all the while chasing down a baseball game that simply refused to be played. Scott always liked the timelessness of baseball. The fact that, in theory, a game could go on forever. There was no game clock to end matters. No tie-breaking procedure. A team had to record 27 outs and, at the end of that ordeal, have more runs that the opponent to be declared a winner. And if there was no winner after nine innings, the game could live in perpetuity.

It wasn't until the past week that Scott realized the idea of a game with no end was more than just a theory. He was riding the infinity loop, the one that only baseball was capable of providing.

"You want the lights out?" Fig asked as he dumped his duffle bag onto the bed.

"Hey Fig," Scott said, pressing up against the glass with his hands cupped over his eyebrows to eliminate the interior glare and recapture at least some of the carefree wonder that he had enjoyed a moment earlier. "How'd we get here?"

"Damned if I know," Fig said, twisting the cap off a Labatt's and taking a mouthful of the highest alcohol content allowable in a brewed beverage this side of the border. "But this is a pretty nice room."

"It's the Honeymoon Suite," Scott said, still trying to block out the ambient light with his hands.

"Only one bed," Fig said.

"Wouldn't be a much of a honeymoon if there were two," Scott answered. "You can have it."

"You sure?" Fig asked politely as he flung his body in the air and plopped down on the mattress without spilling his beer and without waiting for an answer.

"Yeah," Scott said, bristling at JKL's penny-pinching that had led to the shared quarters. "I'll sleep here in this chair. Next to the window."

Fig opened a bag of Doritos, crunched a handful into his mouth, then wiped his nacho-stained hand on the white bedspread.

"Well, we don't have to be at the airport in Toronto until tomorrow afternoon," Fig said, brightly-colored orange flecks of chip spewing from his mouth like dragon brimstone, particularly at the 'haFF to' and 'aFFternoon' sounds. "Wanna play some cards?"

Drip, drip, drip.

"What's that?" Fig asked. His question startled Scott. He was unaware that he'd said it aloud. Maybe he hadn't. Fig had that talent for getting inside his head.

"Drip, drip, drip," Scott said. Or repeated. He still wasn't sure.

Fig cracked open another Labatt's, collected the cards from the tabletop set up next to the window, and jotted down the score from the last hand of gin rummy. Fig had won six straight before Scott finally had gotten on the board with the last hand.

"Two-seventy-four to thirty-six," Fig said. "You deal. What's dripping?"

"That's how it began," Scott said, nodding out the window overlooking the Falls. "Right there. Drip, drip, drip. No one was even around to notice, but they wouldn't have if they were. And it builds and builds and pretty soon it's a stream, then a river. And then it's carving away the earth and lighting the Eastern seaboard and one of the most powerful sights on the planet."

Fig looked over his shoulder and into the bowl.

"You predicting a comeback, Scotty?"

"No," Scott said. "Not in this game. I was just thinking about the question I asked you earlier, about how we got here. To this point. How it began with a few snowflakes. No one could have foreseen the consequences."

Fig grunted thoughtfully.

"For us," Scott continued, "it began before that. Began, and ended, and began again."

The game was scheduled to be played on Tuesday, but JKL wanted his two reporters on the ground ahead of time to write updates on the stadium, the culture and the other colorful dispatches that Scott and Fig would have to churn out. For Scott this was drudgery. He covered baseball. Sports. He wasn't writing travelogues. Fig, though, embraced the assignment wholeheartedly. Writing from the periphery and hitting the subject at the center of the event, that was Fig's strength. He already had a long list of story ideas by the time they had checked into the Niagara Falls hotel, the last room available.

Scott still wasn't sure that the game would be played. Both Brandt and Ott had expressed their displeasure with the idea of playing the game on foreign soil, even though there already had been World Series games in Toronto in years past. What they meant was enemy soil. They both declared that they would not attend the game in Cuba, which was only fitting, given the game was going to be played the same night as the election.

"He's lost all sight of this thing," Felisha told Scott when they spoke on the phone before he'd left for Niagara. "The election, I mean. For 27 months, that was all he focused on, winning the presidency. Now all he cares about is the Red Sox winning the World Series. I swear, I think if the Sox won the game and Ott won the election, he'd be content."

Felisha and Scott had spoken regularly since their face-to-face meeting that night at Magoon's. They weren't back together. Scott made that clear at the end of every conversation. "This doesn't mean anything," he said, clarifying his stance. "OK," Felisha would say. "Good night."

Despite the political impediments to the Havana game, plans went forward. Chicago pitcher Luis Alfredo, who had defected from Cuba on a raft he constructed from broken baseball bats strung together with the yarn from exfoliated baseballs, was even granted assurances from El Presidente himself that he would be allowed to return to the United States after the game. That was a relief for the Cubs; Alfredo was their best lefty out of the bullpen. Had they needed to leave him back in the States to ensure his availability for the coming seasons, it might have been a disadvantage in the game.

Fig had won the game of gin rummy, and the cards and the beers and the scorecards had long been put away. He was lying in the king-sized bed in the Honeymoon Suite flipping from channel to channel and seeing nothing but hockey games -- sometimes the same game from a different broadcast -- while trying to fall asleep.

Scott sat in his chair, staring out at the Falls as he had planned to do. Having experienced his drip-drip-dripipheny about big things starting with small moments, his mind wandered back beyond the few flakes of snow that created the avalanche he currently rode down the mountain slope at a deadly speed.

He started to think about his childhood. About going to college. About meeting Fig and Felisha. About Ryan.

About the first time he couldn't breathe as a fly ball soared toward the gap between the right and center fielders. About the summer nights he had spent crossing out names and trying to follow along with the endless substitutions so he could wind up with a completed scorecard of the All-Star Game. About watching those majestic men tip their caps and wave as they were introduced. Heroes. Gods. Gods in stirrup socks with their pants hitched up high.

He thought about the first time he and Ryan watched a baseball game together, how he'd woken the sleeping 7-month-old up against the wishes of his mother so he could prop the boy on his knee and bounce him to keep those eyes open so he could watch the final outs of the World Series.

He thought about bringing him to Fenway Park and experiencing with Ryan that gasp of disbelief as you come through the chute to find your seats and the lights are bright and there, in the middle of the city, is this field of green and it looks as if it's been there forever, as if the city was built around it, just to preserve that small patch where men play a game. They signed the Pesky Pole that night. They touched the Green Monster. They punched out their All-Star ballot.

They moved down close in the late innings, when most of the fans had left, and Ryan leaned over the wall and was able to grab a handful of dirt from the warning track. He stuffed it into the pocket of his sweatshirt and brought it home and put it into a white legal-sized envelope. "Fenway Park Dirt" was written on the outside in his best grade-school faux calligraphy, as if fancy squiggles and eye-catching angles would make the letters more important and, thus, impart some squiggle-angled importance on its content. That envelope still rested on Ryan's dresser at home.

Scott thought about Ryan leaning over that wall and almost falling onto the field. He was straining so far that his feet came off the ground. Scott lunged forward, but he wasn't able to grab

Ryan in time. He was too far away, having backed up to snap a picture of the event. Someone else anchored him to the practical side of reality. Scott could see the man reach out and wrap his arms around Ryan's waist, secure him, lower him down so he could secure his share of crushed brick and clay from the hallowed ground, and then hoist him back up and tousle his hair with a big smile.

Scott thought about Ryan turning around to see the man who had caught him and helped him.

"Thanks, Uncle Figgy," Ryan had said before turning to his father and smiling.

"Hey Fig," Scott said from his chair beside the window. "You awake?"

"Yup," he said.

"Good," Scott said. "You know I will never forgive you."

Silence.

Had Fig not answered the first question, Scott would have figured him to be passed out in slumber. But for nearly a full minute the second question hung between them. The room was too dark for them to see each other; had the lights been on, they would not have made eye contact, facing in opposite directions as they were. It was a confessional. Two men talking, getting to the bottom of things, discussing bad deeds and betrayals and human frailties and regrets. The regrets of the sinner as well as the regrets of the sinned against mingling in the tense air. Emptying their hearts, but with a screen between them. Only this screen wasn't physical.

Finally, Fig responded.

"I know," he said quietly.

"You never even apologized."

A shorter silence.

"I know."

"I need you to do something for me, Fig. And don't think of this as penance or as a way of making things better or as payback for something. I need you to do something for me tonight. Now. Before we go to sleep. Before we go to Cuba tomorrow. I need you to tell me what happened that night."

"Felisha told you," Fig said.

"I need you to tell me what happened that night," Scott repeated.

"But you already know," Fig said. "My telling you won't change anything."

"Fig," Scott said. "I need you. To tell me. What happened. That night."

CHAPTER EIGHTEEN

He pushed the doorbell once. She answered quickly, before the ding donged.

"I'm here," he said, a little out of breath, pointing out the obvious as the door opened and he slipped through.

"He left me," Felisha told Fig. And she fell into his arms, her tears trickling down the lapel of his suit. Fig wrapped his arms tight around her, letting go just briefly with his left to nudge the door closed and complete the transition from outside to inside. It was an important punctuation. It kept them out. It left them in.

Them. Felisha and Fig.

"Do you want to… talk about it?"

She didn't. She moved away from their embrace and toward the couch, where she sat in front of a half-empty glass of wine that was clearly the most recent in a series of other fully-emptied ones. Fig sat next to her, in front of an empty glass. It wasn't that way for long.

"Did he say why?"

He hadn't.

"You know him better than anyone," Felisha told Fig. "He must have said something to you. Anything. A hint of unhappiness? A whiff of wanderlust?"

"Nothing," Fig said. "Of course, we haven't spoken in a while."

"I know," Felisha said with the first smidgeon of a smile she had been able to muster in days. "You haven't spoken to anyone in a while."

"You were watching?"

"Everyone was," Felisha said. "I even got a call from In-Vogue Magazine asking about you, just like you said I would before you went in."

Fig nodded. He'd been working on his latest project, crashing the reality show "The Real House" as a contestant during its 25th anniversary season. He was posing as a monk who had taken a vow of silence. He spoke not a word. The rest of the "house-mates" went about their lives as wanna-be country singers, re-habbing drug addicts, effeminate heterosexuals, Bible-quoting bullies and over-inflated beach boys. Fig, who never even intro-duced himself and spent most episodes sitting silently in a re-cliner in his boxers and a T-shirt, had become the breakout star of the season. Just as he had predicted.

Before he went into "The Real House," he warned those clos-est to him that they might be hounded by the celebrity press once they figured out his identity.

"I told them I had no idea who you were, just like you asked me to," Felisha said.

"Well, I appreciate that," Fig said. "But that's over. I'm here now. With you."

"And I appreciate *that*," she said. "I just… I had no one else to talk to. No one else who knows me the way you do. That's why I had to text you. I know you said I shouldn't use that number unless it was a dire emergency or if the outside world figured out who you were, but to me, Figgy, to me, this was an emergency. A crisis. I – "

She paused to make sure her words, especially the word she was about to use, got through to him. She leaned in close. She whispered.

"-- I need you."

That word registered with Fig.

"I always told you, Felisha, that if you ever needed anything, I would be there for you," he said. "And I meant it. Obviously. I'm here now. Here for you. But I need you to convince me that this is the right thing to do. Because once we do this, once we make up our minds to go forward with this, there is no going back."

Felisha pulled back just enough to be playful and to give herself enough room to pour another two glasses of wine.

"You ever wonder, Fig?"

"About?" he asked, even though he knew.

"What might have been. If your plan had worked. If Scott and I broke up. Six weeks, right? That was how long it was supposed to last? The plan? If I fell into your arms the way you designed it."

All the time, he wanted to say. You were supposed to be my girl, he wanted to say. This was supposed to be my life, he wanted to say. The family. The kids. The house. The wife. Settled down. Content. Both working, scratching, fighting for whatever edge we could get against the rest of life that was stacked against us but never giving up because our love for each other would not let us, because we had an understanding that we would heave and ho together in the tug-of-war against the world and all the shit that the other side of the rope was anchored with. No stupid traveling to war zones for a story. No sneaking into reality shows for three months at a time. Just a regular job with a regular newspaper doing regular things. Mowing the lawn in the summer, cruising close to the bushes in the side yard where some cold beers were stashed earlier in the day as a reward. Raking the leaves in the fall, making piles for our son and his dog to jump into and spread back around the yard and feigning frustration at having to rake them into a pile a second, third, fourth time. Carving a turkey. Shoveling the driveway. Hanging the Christmas lights and picking out a tree and sneaking the presents under it. The fear of standing together in an emergency room at 4 in the morning. Of not knowing if there will be enough money to pay the mortgage. Of the furnace acting up, the roof leaking, the fridge on the blink. The joy of finding an open spot for a blanket on a crowded beach on a hot day. Of watching a storm move in and counting the gap between lightning and thunder and smelling the sizzling air. Of those wonderful, magical, fleeting nine months that would end with you squeezing my hand until my fingertips turned white and cursing at me for doing this to you and my only response being "I love you." Running to your rescue with a plunger, with a spider-squishing tissue. Encouraging you to take risks. Telling you, in all honesty, no matter the consequences, that yes, those pants make your ass look fat, but doing it so you know that I like fat-looking asses. Attempting to live up to your challenges of being a better person, better husband, better father. Making love, he wanted to say.

All the time, he wanted to say it all.

Maybe it was the previous weeks' silence that had him out of practice at such long speeches, unable to create a connection between the complex images that now rattled around his head -- that had been there for years, since the first day he saw Felisha and foresaw their life together -- and the words that would birth them free from his imagination to reality. Had he said them earlier, much earlier, things might have been different.

Had he said them when Scott and Felisha came to him early in their relationship and told him they were in love, what they thought was truly in love, Scott not even having the nerve to look at him as Felisha did the talking, he might have salvaged some of those wishes.

Had he given voice to them when Scott told him he was going to ask Felisha to marry him, again with eyes staring into the ground, perhaps his dreams would have survived outside the womb of his skull and come true.

If he had jumped at his chance, his last chance, the night before the wedding when Scott was having second thoughts and needed his best man to give him that final nudge to the altar; had he succumbed to his instinct to blow the thing up, to say to hell with it, if I can't have her no one can, certainly not you, my friend, the person I trusted to bring this woman into my life; had he reminded Scott that he was just the bait, the lure, the throw-away crumb that sat on the lip of the unsprung mousetrap Fig had designed with one unseen flaw in it, one God-damned glitch, one loophole; had he given Scott a reason to bolt that night instead of warming his cold feet with empty words spoken through an empty smile; had Scott not looked him in the eyes that night and Fig not seen in those pupils the sight of a broken and crushed Felisha and realized that he could never do that to the woman he loved even if it meant marrying her off to another, then maybe things would have been different.

But Fig had held his tongue for too long. Years. Decades now. The words to describe his emotions had been deleted from his vocabulary like fuzzy pictures from a digital camera, the redacted secrets from a government document. *You ever wonder, Fig?* Christ, it seemed he hadn't wondered about anything else his entire life. And yet the sentences and phrases, the tools he used as a carpenter would his hammer or a doctor his stethoscope, they were pickled inside him. Sealed up tightly. In formaldehyde and vinegar. Crack the jar, let in a little air, and they would rot. They'd been in there too long. They couldn't live outside his mind.

"Two months," was all he muttered. "Max."

"It turned out to be a little longer than that," Felisha said.

"It did," Fig said, clinking her glass.

They sipped.

"Did you bring what I asked you to bring?" Felisha asked.

Fig nodded.

"Can I see it?"

Fig froze. He didn't nod. Didn't shake his head. Didn't smile or frown or smirk or wince. For the first time in his life, Felisha was asking him to do something and he was hesitating.

"It's in my pocket," he finally said. "Let's keep it there for now."

Felisha threw her head back in frustration.

"I want to talk about it before we do this," Fig said.

"I'm so tired of talking," Felisha said, leaning back in close to Fig. "I know what I want."

She slithered next to Fig's ear.

"Give it to me," she hissed.

"You're just upset, Felisha," Fig said, but she raced through his yellow light.

"Give it to me," she said, barely audibly.

"Felisha," Fig said. "No."

"Give it to me."

No sound this time. Just the air pushing out her mouth and the soft click of her tongue as she formed the non-words. Her hand, meanwhile, reached into his pocket and fished around until it found and gripped it. Fig reached down too, grabbing Felisha's wrist.

"Fig," she said, tears welling up again, "I need it. I need you. I need this to end."

Fig released her from his grip and she pulled a small Ziploc bag filled with pills from his pocket. She held it up for a moment to examine it, try to get a feel for how much was in there. It was impossible to make an accurate count. She smiled.

"You sure this is enough?" she asked.

"More than," he said.

"Where'd you get it?"

"The oxy freak," Fig said. "The one supposed to be rehabbing. She had it stashed in the house."

Felisha put the bag on the table next to the wine glasses.

"Is there enough ... for two?"

Fig nodded.

"To get the job done?"

Nod.

"And by job I mean ..."

Nod.

"Good," she said.

They sat staring at the bag.

"Well," Felisha finally said, shattering the quiet, "I guess this is it."

"A toast?" Fig said.

Felisha chuckled, then rebalanced her composure with the seriousness of their business.

"OK," she said, and handed him his wine glass while keeping her own. "Um, well, I've never been good at speeches ..."

She began to cry again.

"... but I guess I just want to say that I'm sorry. I'm sorry things didn't work out, you know? Not with us, but with, just, everything. I'm sorry I was lazy sometimes. I'm sorry I worked too hard at other times. And I'm not scared now, Fig."

Bubbles began to flow from her nose.

"I know what I'm doing is drastic, what we're doing is crazy. Or seems crazy. But we get each other, Fig. We know there is no other way. That we can't go backward, and going forward will be too painful. That this is the only way. To end it."

She sniffled through her weeping and flipped her hair from her face.

"You know, I never read a book with a good ending. I never got to the back of a novel and felt satisfied. I was always sad. These characters become a part of my life for 200 or 300 pages and you know, you just know, that as the number of pages behind them dwindles, their lifespan is shrinking too. I always felt like I was finally getting to know them and then, I don't know, no more pages. But now I don't feel that way. This feels complete. This feels like the right time to end things. To stop reading."

"There may be some pages after this," Fig said.

"I know," she said. "There will be pages for others to read. I'm not interested in them. I've known these characters for too long. It's time."

"Well," Fig said. "So much for not being good at speeches."

They laughed.

"I'll just say," Fig added to the toast, "to what might have been."

They clinked glasses and reached into the bag for a pinch of pills each and shoved them into their mouths like M&Ms or potato chips, chasing them down with the rest of the glass of wine.

"How many?" Scott said, interrupting the story for the first time.

"Three," Fig said. "Just enough to knock her on her naive ass, give her a headache in the morning."

"And you took three too?"

"I did."

"When they did the blood work at the hospital, they said she had swallowed about 50 pills," Scott said.

"I know," Fig told him in the darkness of the Niagara Falls Honeymoon Suite. "She took three while I was there. She was asleep. I carried her into her bed -- your bed -- your old bed, I guess, technically -- and I laid her down and pulled the covers over her and she was asleep, Scott. I even rolled her on her side in case, you know. I kissed her on the forehead and held her hand and made sure she was still breathing. And then I left."

"You left."

'I fucking left, yeah," he said.

"And you have no idea what happened after that?"

"I know now," Fig said.

"Tell me," Scott said. "Tell me."

"I left the house but the bag of pills was still on the table. She knew I was full of crap when I told her three pills would do the job. So after I left she got up from the bed where she had been acting as if she was asleep, passed out, and swallowed the rest of them. Her stomach was so bloated with wine from choking them down that she threw them up. She had to rinse them off, Scott, crawl on the floor of the bathroom and pick them up and rinse the vomit off of them and re-swallow them with a glass of milk to keep them down."

"And who found her?"

"Scott, you know who found her."

"Tell me."

Fig sat quietly for a moment.

"Ryan did."

"Ryan did," Scott said. "Unforgivable."

"Scott, I had no idea he was home. I had no idea she'd try to off herself with her kid -- your kid -- in the room down the hallway. Why would she do that?"

"Do you know how he found her?"

"Yes."

"Convulsing."

"Yes."

"Vomiting. On her back. So she was choking."

"Yes."

"Overdosing on pills that you gave his mother so she could kill herself."

"Yes."

"He called 9-1-1."

"I know."

"Had to describe what he was seeing. Describe his mother in that situation."

"Yes."

"There's a tape of it, did you know that? A tape of the 9-1-1 call. They keep them for every call, and all you have to do is know someone who works there and they can fish out the particular call you are looking for. I did that, Fig. I fished out that call. He's a child and he's answering questions about his mother as she is dying in front of him. Told by the operator to push her onto her side and put his hand in her mouth so he could clear out the vomit. You put him through that."

"I know."

Neither of them came close to falling asleep in the still-dark room. Even the colorful illumination on the Falls had been extinguished for the night, but the spotlight on the powerful eroding force that had been cutting a horseshoe between the two men for the last several years still burned bright in the room.

"I can never forgive you," Scott said. "Never."

"You keep saying that," Fig said.

"I mean it."

"I know you do."

"How do you know that?" Scott asked. "How can you be so certain?"

"Because," Fig said, "I haven't forgiven you either."

"What are you talking about?" Scott asked as dawn was about to rise on a sleepless but otherwise silent night. Hours had passed since they last spoke aloud, with Scott's mind focusing not on Cuba or the Cubs or baseball or deadlines or lawsuits but on going over every step of his relationship with Felisha. "You're the one who was pushing us together. You're the one who is still pushing us together."

"To make her happy," Fig said. "God knows why *you* would make her happy. But you do. So I do it for her."

"I never loved her like that," Scott said, shaking his head.

"You don't even love yourself, Scott. I wouldn't expect you to know how to love someone else."

"What does that mean?"

There was no answer. There didn't have to be. They both knew.

"So?" Scott said. "Why do you love Felisha?"

"Because she excites me."

"Don't be gross."

"Excites me spiritually. She drives me. She makes me work for her smiles, for her acknowledgments. Because when I see her happy, it gives me a high that I never want to end for either of us, and when I see her in pain, it destroys me to the point that I'll go to any length to erase the source of her discomfort. Because she is beautiful and sexy but also comfortable and cozy. Because she is welcoming, but not a pushover; accommodating but not easy. Because she gets stressed about little things but is strong enough to handle the big ones. Mostly. Because she thinks she knows what she wants and can be so foolish about that, whether it's wanting you or wanting to off herself that night or wanting that clown she's working for to win the election. Because she needs me even though she may not recognize it all the time, but deep down in her heart, she knows that I will always be there for her. Because I disgust myself when I lie to her, and she's the only person in the world that makes me feel that way, and she's been the target of some of my biggest lies. 'You two make a great couple.' Or 'I'm so happy for you both.' You made me give a toast on your fucking wedding day, Scott, a day of vows and oaths and forever holding your peace, and you made me stand up and lie. I guess I always knew I'd have to do that at some point. I knew that I could never be completely honest with her. Because from the first moment I saw her, I knew that she was the woman for me. And it killed me that, no matter how hard I tried, I would not be the man for her. That's what love is, Scott. That's what you're missing. God bless you, I think, sometimes, because it's agonizing. But then I feel bad for you because you had it all and it didn't even register. What's worse? Knowing heaven exists and never being able to get in? Or someone else getting in and having it mean so little to them?"

"Being with Felisha is not heaven," Scott said.

"So what is heaven, Mr. Findle, philosopher of your age?"

Scott looked out the window. The rising sun was just starting to touch the rushing water as it broke over the lip of the Falls. He wondered if that river had any awareness of its greatness. Some water droplets are destined for little more than puddles. Some are lucky enough to be part of a lake or, if there are enough of them, an ocean. But there are others, the truly special ones, that gather in places like this. And while there are not as many of them as form the Pacific and they are not as important as the ones that bring life to the African Savannah or fall in the Amazon jungles or even span the 90 miles from the United States to Cuba, they are the ones people remember. The ones that shoot out of the geysers in Yosemite. The ones that carved the canyons of the southwest. Even the ones that are fired into the air outside the mammoth casinos in Las Vegas.

He pictured himself joining those molecules of water that had converged at just the right time in just the right place to forge such a mighty current. Together they shaped the landscape around them. All these little drops acting together. Flowing together from the Great Lake down through the valley until finally, with one last push, they spill over and people gape and gasp. The same water a mile away in either direction is nondescript, unimportant, insignificant. But for that brief moment when it tumbles and sprays, it is a wonder.

"I guess," Scott said, "my idea of heaven is ... making a splash. Doing something wondrous, unexpected, even if it's just for an instant. Being remembered for just one great thing. One stroke that no one would have thought possible. One note that was thought to be unreachable. One act, swift and defining, that would last beyond my lifetime."

"So what's stopping you?"

CHAPTER NINETEEN

Scott pointed to the picture behind the bar, the face he had stared at so many nights during spring training nights in Fort Myers.

"Did you know he wanted to change journalism?"

"Change it?" The Professor asked, sipping his Dewar's.

"Just the way he changed how cars were produced. I did a little reading on Henry Ford this winter. He wanted to create an assembly line for creating stories and articles. He even started his own magazine to put the theory into practice. It was called *The Independent.* One person would report the facts. Another would add the quotes. The next guy down the line would add some humor, if it was called for. Or some emotion. Depending on what they wanted the tone of the article to be. Finally, the headline was assembled like headlamps on a Model T and the story came off the line."

"How'd that work out?"

"Not too good," Scott said. "Especially when he inserted himself into the process. His job was to affix the anti-Semitic slant."

"I heard," The Professor said, "that Henry Ford was mentioned favorably in 'Mein Kampf' and that Hitler kept a framed photo of Ford on his wall."

"Is that right?" Scott said, sipping his beer. "The other guy there, Edison, now he was a hard worker. One percent inspiration, ninety-nine percent perspiration and all that. Working in his lab all those hours, filing all those patents. Ford? He was going to be a farmer but quit because it was too hard. He didn't like the work. That's how he got into engines and motorized vehicles, because he didn't want to do the pushing and pulling himself. Such different approaches. And yet look at them. Two buddies. Two titans. Standing there in front of their vacation homes in Florida."

"There's always people who are trying to change the world," The Professor said. "They do it in different ways. In different scopes and scales. But things change and it's fellas like them that generally do the pushing. You just have to hope they know where they're going."

Scott nodded, tapping his plastic hotel pen on the brass railing of the bar at Gator Bites Tail and Ale, creating a pleasing ping. He thought about the changes in his own world during the last year, since he had left Fort Myers with the Red Sox to embark on the damndest season he'd ever covered. He thought about the changes during the last three months, since baseball declared the championship undecided, since Brandt won the election. Since he called up that nurse from down here, Jessica, and she remembered him.

"You don't forget something like that," she chuckled when he approached her.

He thought about the first day he entered the very same bar where he sat now, the craziness with which he exited the building then, and how every day of work since felt as if he was grabbing the job by its nuts -- and it his -- just to stop the bleeding.

He thought about the changes in himself. How he'd grown. Stood up for himself. Made his own decisions. Found what made him happy. His friends. Ryan. Baseball. Baseball like when he was a kid. He'd even stopped marking the time of certain happenings, and simply enjoyed them.

He wondered who had been doing the pushing in all of that. Himself? Fig? Felisha? The Commissioner? The networks? Maybe they all had a shoulder leaning into it. Maybe they were on an assembly line, focusing on their little piece of the process. But did any of them know where they were going?

"They should leave well enough alone," Scott laughed at the pushers.

The Professor raised his glass in agreement.

Scott never made it to Cuba, but that was just fine because no one else had, either. Well, no one but Fig. He left on that flight from Toronto all alone. Scott flew south from Toronto that day too, but he went only as far as Florida. By way of Boston. Where he picked up Ryan.

"What about the World Series?" Ryan asked when he was told they were leaving.

"It'll have to go on without me," he said.

He was wrong.

The teams never made it to Cuba to play Game Seven. The Department of Defense had ordered a naval blockade of the island nation with the intention of keeping the players out, a token gesture that baseball planned to avoid simply by flying over the floating arsenal and daring the U.S. warships to shoot down U.S. charter planes filled with U.S. millionaires and U.S. celebrities. But that showdown never took place.

El Presidente died in his sleep the night before the teams were set to arrive (with Fig at his bedside, of course). His brother, who had taken leadership of the country a decade earlier when the old revolutionary's health began to falter, canceled the World Series events and called for a national week of mourning. It would have been a touching tribute to *El Presidente* to play the game in his honor, in his memory. But while his brother shared his anti-imperialist zeal and love of camouflage clothing, he did not share El Presidente's appreciation for *beisbol*. Brother was all too happy to avoid hosting the game, and saw it as his own way of sticking it to the Americans. Besides, *Estadio Latinoamericano* would be needed for El Presidente to lie in state as the anticipated millions of mourners would be encouraged to pay their final respects.

JKL was pissed when Scott disappeared on the verge of Game Seven, but he quickly got over the disappointment when Fig began churning out more award-winning stories from Cuba. It also helped to assuage his anger that Game Seven never took place. Soon the country had its headlines grabbed by other spectacles and conflicts. There were other stories on which to focus. Other turmoils to chronicle. The NFL season rolled in. There was a scandal at a prominent college football program where coeds had offered sexual favors to replay officials in exchange for overturned calls. The Yankees, moving right into the offseason despite the lack of a conclusion to the actual season, signed the first openly gay pitcher in the major leagues ... from Japan. Life moved on. Scott was as surprised as anyone.

"I went online last month and there was hardly any mention of the Series," Scott said. "I was a little... disappointed. And relieved. It was weird."

"You know how these stories flare up and then burn out," The Professor said.

Scott nodded. Some scorch brightly, briefly across the sky, then run out of fuel as quickly as they appeared. Others, Scott thought, smolder for years before exploding. Like the one between Fig and himself. In both cases, he now realized, the burn was finite. Ultimately, it cooled.

"Remember when all we heard about was that plane that crashed somewhere in the ocean?" The Professor continued.

"Every day for two weeks. And then? When was the last time you heard anything about that?"

"Good point," Scott said. "Guess you just have a different perspective of the diminishing national attention span when you find yourself in the middle of it. And then out of it."

Hardly anyone noticed when The Commissioner declared the season over in early December. Most thought it already had been completed -- or at least abandoned -- but the death certificate had to be signed by The Commissioner to finalize the proceedings and allow teams to begin anew. Contracts, free agency, options, they were all tied to the end of the World Series. Until it was over – or, technically, not ever going to happen – all of those machinations were in limbo. The paper ran a short wire story on it.

Pretty soon, it seemed to Scott, they were back in spring training, sitting at the bar in Fort Myers, talking about baseball and life and not paying much attention to the lack of a champion.

"What'd you get Jessica for Valentine's Day?" asked The Professor.

"Candy and flowers," Scott said.

"You can do better than that!" called a voice from the door of the bar.

"Figgy!" Scott yelled. "What are you doing here?"

"Just came to say hello and I knew I'd find you two here," Fig said. "JKL's got me working on a story about corruption in the charter fishing boat industry down here."

"Pull up a stool!"

"You two buddies again?" The Professor whispered to Scott as Fig made his way toward them. "I thought it was unforgivable?"

"It was," Scott said, instinctively looking for the watch that he no longer wore. "But we reached an agreement."

Fig told his friends about Cuba. About covering *El Presi-*

dente's funeral. About how he had at first been accused of assassinating the man but was quickly cleared and asked to eulogize him at the funeral. "A miscommunication," Fig said, without pinning that description on a particular part of the story.

Scott told Fig about the new stadium in Boston, which he'd been given a tour of before coming south with the team. It had been completed just weeks earlier, and only $1.2 billion over budget. He told him about Jessica and Ryan getting to know each other. He outlined for Fig the premise of his new website, www.ninefortysix.com, which was dedicated to creative writing about baseball. Poems, haikus, long-form non-fiction, short stories. As long as it was about baseball – actual baseball – and not the business of or the politics of or the shortcomings of the game. He'd asked and was surprised to have gotten Roger Angell to write the second story posted on the site, ironically a look at all of the dramatic Game Sevens in World Series history.

Scott had written the first, about the most beautiful baseball call he'd ever heard. He named the website after the story.

"It's named after 9:46 p.m.," Scott explained.

Fig looked blank.

"That's the time Vin Scully mentions in the Koufax call."

Right.

"*I would think that the mound at Dodger Stadium right now is the loneliest place in the world,*" Scott said, reciting the Scully lines as if they were Shakespeare. Only better.

"*On the scoreboard in right field it is 9:46 p.m. in the City of the Angels, Los Angeles, California. And a crowd of twenty-nine thousand one-hundred thirty nine just sitting in to see the only pitcher in baseball history to hurl four no-hit, no-run games,*" Scott continued. "*And Sandy Koufax, whose name will always remind you of strikeouts, did it with a flurry. He struck out the last six consecutive batters. So when he wrote his name in capital letters in the record books, that 'K' stands out even more than O-U-F-A-X.*"

The three sat in reverence.

Scott opened his phone to show some preliminary designs for the logo, and told him how JKL had taken the news of his resignation. Because he now lived in Florida, Scott offered to pitch in on spring training coverage when he could. And, he told JKL, if something like Game Seven ever came up again and he wanted to pull him back into the circus as he had done to The Professor, don't bother, because he would have already changed his phone number.

They laughed at the Cubs, who were content to raise the banner for the National League pennant and were so proud of not losing the World Series that they were going to wear patches on their shoulders all season commemorating the end of baseball's longest losing streak, even if they didn't actually win anything to stop the skid.

After he lost the election, Ott bought the team from ChiLock. Or rather took it after the company had embezzled $735 million from his campaign. Ott didn't seem to mind losing the election; he was much happier running the Cubs than the country. Another lovable loser. They seemed to fit together well. His first act as owner was to stop the hideous construction that was defacing Wrigley Field. His second was to petition the City Council to amend the rules regarding the use of lights at the ballpark. By outlawing them.

They chuckled about their adventures, reliving their journey. All those flights. All those almosts. All those bylines and deadlines and datelines and sources and columns and newsers and stresses. And for what?

For no game.

"How's Felisha?" Scott asked Fig.

"Good," he said. "Better. She understood."

She'd even gotten Scott a present. As a high-ranking member of the Administration, she'd convinced President Brandt to extend permanent citizenship to Szczesny. In exchange, of course, for dropping the libel suit. It went against everything Brandt stood for in terms of both immigration and baseball, but he was described as "merciful" and "magnanimous" in the papers, so those wounds healed quickly.

"There's just one thing I haven't been able to figure out," Scott said as they finished retracing their steps.

"Who are you, Velma from Scooby-Doo?" Fig quipped.

"No, I just can't for the life of me figure out what happened with the election."

"Brandt won," The Professor said.

"I know. I mean the first election. The real Election Day. The one that didn't take place. How could the Secret Service lose two presidential candidates? And why did the Chief Justice of the Supreme Court postpone the election?"

"Hmm," hmmed The Professor with the nonchalance of both spring training and a writer who had returned to retirement, as if one ever truly stops being a reporter.

The three stared less than curiously, blankly even, at the pictures behind the bar, sipping their drinks, letting their light and easy spring training waves float in their heads, soft fly ball thoughts fungoed against the clear blue sky, not a care between them.

"Funny thing," Fig told Scott. "I used to play golf with this judge."

In 1874, Colonel W.W. Graves decided that Fort Lewis was no place to raise his family. The decorated Civil War hero had become one of the first ranching tycoons in West Texas, a founding father of the cattle industry (when he wasn't busy as a famous Indian fighter, that is). He had no qualms about shedding the blood of a herd of cattle or a tribe of Comanches or even turning a game of poker into a shootout, as he was known on occasion to do. And he had no problems with the gamblers and gunslingers and women of disrepute who inhabited the booming town of Fort Lewis; in fact, he had done business with and befriended many of them, often, in the case of the ladies, at the same time.

What he could not abide, however, was the rescinding of a law that had made it punishable by fine and possible imprisonment in the newly constructed jailhouse to expectorate within town limits. The Colonel found the act of relieving one's self of the liquid contents of one's mouth a vile and revolting habit. For many years, he alone policed the streets of Fort Lewis in regard to that otherwise unenforced doctrine, making citizen's arrests whenever he encountered what he described in his journal as "one of those chaw-chomping scoundrels whose tar-soaked phlegm and saliva spewed from their wretched cheeks." He'd even shot and killed an unlucky violator of the town's creed whose oral ejection had landed on the top of the left boot of the good Colonel. That the bottom of that same article of footwear was caked in the remnants of his slain cattle, that the man had just been urinating on the side of the bank that Colonel Graves recently had purchased, and that the man was the recently-elected mayor of Fort Lewis seemed to make little difference. Graves drew his pistol and cut the man down for spitting, wiping the stain from his boot across the unflinching face of the scoundrel.

Graves fought to keep the law on the books, but the townspeople found it bad for business to be constantly fining and locking up and, every so often, executing without trial the cowboys and frontiersmen who frequented the saloons, whorehouses and other establishments. So when the regulation was wiped clean from the town's charter like the dribble that clung to the lips of those one-time lawbreakers, Colonel Graves knew what had to be done.

He packed his wife and 13 children into a stagecoach and headed 85 miles to the west, where he established his own town. There was no room in the coach to bring any of their property, so the Graves family left their entire estate behind in Fort Lewis but except for one treasure that the Colonel carried on his lap during the journey as he drove the horses ahead of the wagon. Made of the brightest silver, engraved with his name --

To Col. W.W. Graves
From a Grateful Nation
U.S. Army

-- it was, agreed all who saw it, the finest cuspidor that had ever been fashioned. And when it came time to name his new town, Graves could think of only one suitable designation.

"And thus," the old woman at the desk of the Chamber of Commerce said, "we welcome you to Spittoon, Texas. Population: Two thousand, three hundred and nine."

"Fascinating story," Scott said half-heartedly. Jessica smacked him playfully on the shoulder for being rude.

"Unfortunately, the spittoon was just recently stolen from Town Hall. Biggest crime here in 25 years. So I can't direct you to what's normally our biggest tourist attraction. What brings y'all here, if I may ask?" the woman drawled. "We don't get many visitors."

The two didn't quite know.

They arrived on the insistence of Fig O'Leary, who had planned a romantic getaway for the new couple – a few days in the country, he called it – in early January just before the start of spring training.

"Well," the woman said, pushing back from the desk and unsure what to make of their inability to answer the question, "There's a Holiday Inn just around the corner. Head two blocks down and when you get to the flashing red light, stop …"

She paused here to illustrate how long they should stop.

"… then when there is no other traffic, turn right. The hotel will be on the left."

"Thank you!" Jessica chirped with excitement.

"Yeah, thanks," Scott said, swirling a mouth full of saliva and leaning forward to expel it with his tongue through the small gap in his front teeth before another whack from Jessica forced him to swallow it with a loud gulp.

"Enjoy your stay in Spittoon!"

Shortly after college, when he dabbled with the idea of writing fiction but found that he didn't have the imagination to make it as a novelist or short story author, that his talent for writing lay more in describing actual events than fictitious ones, Scott had written a half of a tale about a computer engineer who was able to hack into the GPS of cars. Expensive cars, mostly. The drivers would punch in a desire to go to the opera or a museum or some other high-class endeavor and the main character would take over the navigation system. Before long the dapper couple would be driving through the worst parts of town. "Are you sure this is right?" the wife would ask. "I'm just following the directions," hubby would respond. "Maybe this is a shortcut." Eventually the car would be led to a dead end, where a half dozen hoodlums would emerge, box the car in, strip it of its valuables – radios, CD players, hub caps, rims, of course the GPS – and relieve the couple of their jewelry and cash. They'd call the police. "What were you doing in that neighborhood to begin with?" the cops would say to the well-breds, suspicious that the couple had been looking for drugs or other forms of illicit fun.

Scott felt like one of those couples as he followed his own GPS out of what served as Downtown Spittoon and drove along the dusty, desolate road. It felt as if he and Jessica were the only human inhabitants for hundreds of miles even though they had just pulled out of the Holiday Inn.

"If I didn't know Fig any better, I'd think this was an ambush," Jessica said, apparently thinking thoughts similar to Scott's even though she'd never read his short story. This, Scott thought, might just work out.

"I do know Fig better," Scott said, "and I still think this might be an ambush."

"Are you sure you have the right place?" Jessica asked as the landscape grew more and more devoid of life.

"I think so," Scott said. "He was very specific about this location and particularly the time. He wanted us to be there by 2 o'clock."

"But he didn't say why?"

"Of course not," Scott said.

"Do you want to turn around?" Jessica asked, giving him an out.

"No," Scott sighed. "No. It seemed very important to him."

"Spittoon," Jessica said several times under her breath as they drove along the unpaved roads. "Spittoon. Spittoon. Who would steal a spittoon?"

Scott was about to offer up a guess but was interrupted by Jessica.

"There!"

She pointed to an area on the side of the road where about a dozen other cars were parked.

"That must be it."

"It must be," Scott said, "but I still don't know what 'it' is."

They pulled in and parked. Not a soul could be seen. Just miles of brush in three directions and, to their right, to the north, a grove of tall blue oaks that were the only impediment to a 360-degree view of the horizon. They exited the car.

"This is the place," Scott said, triple-checking the coordinates that Fig had given him.

"Hello!" Jessica hollered through her cupped hands. "Anyone! Hello!"

They listened for a response. Nothing but the buzz of insects and the breeze floating across the tops of the grasses answered.

"What is this?" Jessica asked Scott.

"Shhh!" he hushed her.

"Do you hear someone?"

"Shhh!" he said louder, more emphatically.

He hunched over, hanging his head, facing the ground with his eyes closed to dull his other senses and heighten his hearing.

"There," he said. "Did you hear that?"

"No."

"Listen again."

This time Jessica joined in the blind search for sound.

"There," Scott said.

"I heard it," Jessica said. "A soft click. A snap. Like someone walking across dried kindling, but very slowly. One step every few seconds."

"Where is it coming from?" Scott asked, then answered his own question when he heard it next. "There. From the oaks."

"It's probably just a jackrabbit hopping through the woods," Jessica said. "Or the wind knocking the limbs together."

"No," Scott said. "I know that sound. There's only one way to make that sound. And it's not with oak. It's with ash. And leather."

Scott marched deliberately toward the trees and Jessica followed behind. The clicking grew louder, until it was more a crack. Scott paused in front of the oaks for a moment, listened intently, then stepped into the grove. For fifty yards or so, he meandered through the trunks, over the roots, through the branches. All the while, the cracks grew louder and more distinct, until finally he emerged from the mini-forest into a clearing and found ... a diamond.

"He's here!" Fig yelled, and the men around him seemed excited by the news.

Scott still was too far away to make out exactly what was happening, but he recognized Fig's voice and began to walk toward the area where a baseball field was positioned. It seemed to be a high school field, but certainly with no high school nearby.

A chain link fence surrounded the playing area. The dugouts weren't dug out, just benches positioned down each baseline. A stand of wooden bleachers hovered behind first and again behind third.

As Scott walked closer, he started to make out some details of the field. The shabby but defined grass on the infield. The worn-out areas in the pasture where the outfielders habitually stood. Closer still, he could recognize the forms of the men throwing baseballs casually and playing pepper. They wore long baseball shorts with pulled-up socks so their legs would be mostly covered during slides, allowing just a peek of knee flesh to show. And T-shirts. Cotton T-shirts, half of them in gray, the other half in white to designate the team they belonged to.

The faint clicks that he had heard from the parking area now were the thunderous cracks of batting practice, the sound bouncing off the surrounding trees that hid the field from view, echoing thunder in a valley.

There was Morris Oates. And Spooner LaRoche. And over there, warming up his pitching arm, was Daryl Hoyt.

Scott finally reached the fence behind home plate, an arching screen of intertwined metal that went straight up and then stretched out toward the field to keep foul balls within a respectable boundary.

"What is this?" Scott asked, reaching for Jessica's hand. "Fig, what is this?"

"It's Game Seven."

Scott squeezed Jessica's hand so tightly that she squealed.

"The guys got tired of all of the politics and economics and bullshit getting in the way, so we decided to get together here and settle this thing without the networks or media or corporate owners," Fig said. "Just baseball. Out in the open. Free. The way it's supposed to be played."

"Like when we were kids," Jimmy Grouper added as he walked past.

Scott smiled.

"You did this, Figgy?"

"Well," he replied, "I had a little help."

Scott looked around at the field. It was far from meeting big league specifications, with crabgrass and uneven dirt. But the important parts seemed to be measured to perfection. Ninety feet between the bases. Sixty and a half feet to the pitcher's rubber, which sat atop an island mound of clay. He looked down the third base line, onto the Red Sox bench, and saw that the batboy was waving to him. Scott waved back.

"You brought Ryan," Scott said softly to Fig.

"He was the little help," Fig said. "It was actually his idea. He thought it would make you happy."

"But why here? Why Spittoon?"

"Because," Fig said, "anywhere else and this place would be crawling with reporters and cameras. It had to be somewhere no one would look for it. Somewhere no one would think to even come upon."

"We were just in town," Jessica said. "This certainly qualifies."

"We even have a trophy for the winner," said Cubs catcher Boone Flanagan, walking past with Col. W.W. Graves' prized silver urn under his arm, dropping a mouthful into it.

"And the best part," Fig said, thumping the chest protector he was wearing under his shirt, "is I get to be the umpire!"

"You? An arbiter of justice? Ha!" Scott said with a smile.

"There is one condition," Fig warned Scott.

Scott stepped backward.

"I have to forgive you? I told you, I can't. I've tried. I cannot."

"No, no, no," Fig says. "I know. But you have to promise

that you won't write what happens here. It's all off the record. No mention, ever, of who wins, who loses, who has the big hit, who strikes out whom. Ever. The only people who will know which team wins the World Series are standing here in this meadow right now."

"That means no stupid questions, either," Casper Gulligan said as he trotted out to coach third. "No 'Why'd you pull him?' or 'Why didn't you pinch hit for him?' or 'Why'd you wave him home?'"

Scott looked around. Everything he loved was in front of him. Ryan. Baseball in its purest form. Jessica, though he had yet to come to terms with that reality. And even, in a strange and complicated way, Fig.

"The boys are heading down to spring training tomorrow, so you'd better make up your mind quickly," Fig said. "The game goes on with or without you. You want to stay and watch, you have to keep mum. Do we have a deal?"

Scott silently took Jessica's arm and escorted her to the top row of the wooden bleachers just beyond the third base line.

"Look, they even got me a beer," Scott said, pointing to the large cup waiting for him.

"What? No!" Fig said. "That's not a beer. That's Buster. Or what's left of him."

Jessica insisted the remains be moved to the opposite set of bleachers, but Scott argued that Buster would never sit there on the first base side to root for the Cubs. A compromise was reached. Buster Sinclair was handed over the chain link fence and placed on the Red Sox bench. It was, Scott noted to himself, a perch that was all too familiar to the backup outfielder and one that, had he been rightfully situated on that night in Chicago, likely would have spared his life and all the chaos that followed his demise.

With the ashes removed from the bleachers, Scott took his own seat, just high enough to have an elevated view over the team's bench but close enough to hear the players talking to Ryan, admiring his batting stance, giving him pointers, enlisting him to come down the line to help the left fielder warm up his arm between innings.

The players had come to their benches from their pregame routines. Hoyt trotted in from the makeshift bullpen, which, in these parts, might have actually been a pen for bulls at one point. He toweled off his face and took a sip of water from the cooler that hung on the fence. Scott was in the perfect vantage point to root for a baserunner to hit a triple or go first-to-third on a hit-and-run and come barreling toward him before flopping headfirst onto the bag.

"Do we have a deal?" Fig asked again, just to make sure.

There were no lights. No television cameras. No thunderous announcements. No walk-up music. No between-innings proposals, no sponsors painted on the walls, no out-of-town scores, no blooper reels. Just quiet baseball in all its pastoral perfection, no more glamorous than it was when Abner Doubleday himself was nursing the game to life and hammering out the rules. Under the sun. On the grass and the dirt.

Scott gave the field one last surveillance through his teared-up eyes and choked out two words from his hoarse, emotional throat.

"Batter up."

ACKNOWLEDGMENTS

This will be a little shocking for a lot of people.

So many folks offered encouragement and support during the process of writing this book and had very little idea they were doing so. I dare say the vast majority had no clue that I was even working on a novel. Some would have thought me incapable of doing so had they known. Others probably would be shocked to know that I'd be interested in reading one, much less writing one. And yet, in casual contact, they helped pull me through the process.

I want to thank the newspaper writers I work with and against, some of whom I see on a daily basis and get to travel the country with, others who I keep in touch with only through the liking of each other's tweets. While we are competitors, we manage to have a close relationship and I thank you all for that, especially Paul Schwartz, Art Stapleton, Ralph Vacchiano, Ebenezer Samuel, Bill Pennington, Steve Serby; and my long-distance crew of Jenny Vrentas, Kimberley Martin, Ohm Youngmisuk, Mike Garafolo, Kim Jones and Judy Battista. Know it or not, you have all been a sounding board for me, a source of ideas, and a fantastic audience for trying out material in a safe setting.

I thank Mike Rose and Hank Winnicki at Newsday for being nothing like the editors portrayed in this book. You give me space and have confidence in my judgment and abilities without feeling the need to babysit. I appreciate that. While I'm in Melville, thank you too to Jeff Weinberg and the others who man (or woman!) the copy desk and make sure I don't look like an idiot when the paper comes out the next day. You have made me look like a better writer than I am on many occasions. An easy job, I'm sure, but one I appreciate. Greg Gutes in particular has helped me sharpen my craft and his detailed work on this project was invaluable.

My colleagues Bob Glauber and Neil Best have had a tremendous influence on me. We have been on the other end of each other's bitch sessions time and again, but after each of them we always remember we are professionals and we go back to work. There are no people I would rather do that with side-by-side than you two. As Hyman Roth says: "This is the business we've chosen."

Now, on to those who knew about *Game Seven* and helped push it along. The novel had no bigger champion than Tracey Menzies, and that was before she even knew a thing about it. It was her foot that kicked me in the ass and got me to writing. For that I will forever be grateful. Your faith in me was more than I had in myself. And I have a lot. Quite literally, there would be no *Game Seven* without you.

Thanks to John DiMeola, who read early versions of the project and offered compelling arguments for fixes along with compassion for a fellow writer stuck in a regular life. He also allowed me to crib some lines from an earlier project we worked on many lifetimes ago. One day that project will be available for viewing in a theater near you.

Thanks to Tom Ferrara, who helped design the cover in exchange for payment in the form of liquid assets. On the rocks.

Thanks to Marshall Cohen, who helped me figure out how to stop a presidential election, no easy task even for Fig O'Leary. I'll thank you personally on the Saturday before the Super Bowl in perpetuity! Thanks to all of the editors and agents who took to the time to read even a page of this project before it was published. Hopefully one day I can have a drink with all of you – one at a time! – and say "I told you so."

In 2003, the Cubs and Red Sox were both in the playoffs and my father came to me with an idea: *What if those two teams were to meet in a World Series that nobody wins?* At the time, neither franchise had won a championship in almost a century. When the Red Sox did win, I thought the idea had died. Then the Cubs became good. And Cuba was opened. But in writing, there is always a way.

My wife, Amanda, helped me find it. She tolerated the laptop on the kitchen table, the empty whiskey glasses in the sink in the morning, and the long process of reading and editing everything. Every snippet, every scene, every chapter, every version. Right away, dropping her own work to take a look at mine. She vowed to stick with me for better or worse on our wedding day, but she did not promise to like everything I wrote. I'm glad she didn't. Her critical thoughts weren't always accepted, but they were appreciated.

So, a thousand zillion thank-yous to the two people who helped form me and this book: My father, who planted the seed, and Amanda, who put up with a decade of fertilizer for it!

ABOUT THE AUTHOR

Tom Rock is an award-winning sports journalist for *Newsday* in New York, where he has worked since 1996 and covered the NFL since 2006. His articles have been cited in the 2005 edition of *The Best American Sports Writing* and recognized by the APSE (Associated Press Sports Editors), New York Press Club, Press Club of Long Island, and the New York City Chapter of the Society of Professional Journalists. He has over 13,000 followers on Twitter – some of whom even appreciate his zany analysis of sports and life – and is a frequent guest on New York sports radio.

Tom lives in Sound Beach, New York, with his wife, Amanda, and their three children.

Game Seven is his first novel.

30278221R00161